Apocalyptic Winter

— Book 1 —

An Angry Eagle Anthology

A.R. Maloney
Dennis Welton—Theresa Shaver
Albert Moss — C.A. Moll — Susan Isenberg
Christi Reed — N.A. Broadley
DJ Cooper — D. Stalter
Stephanie Mylchreest

Angry Eagle Publishing

https://AngryEaglePublishing.com

CONTENTS

Apocalyptic Winter

Cover Artwork by Vitaly S. Alexius & Anton Churunov

www.rom.ac

—

Finding many of these wonderful writers is as easy as finding your way into the social groups on Facebook.
Check them out
Written Apocalypse
https://Facebook.com/groups/writtenapocalypse
Women of the Apocalypse
https://www.facebook.com/groups/WomenoftheApocalypse

Apocalyptic Winter

FORWARD

The authors were given a prompt

—

"One of the most challenging things about an apocalyptic tale is the weather. Can you describe an apocalyptic event from the perspective of winter survival? Will your characters be miserable, or will they be joyful? Is there happiness or will it only show the misery?"

The choices are up to the authors on a few conditions:

All of the following words must be included in the story

★Christmas Tree★

★Serving Spoon★

★Bear★

★Secret★

Apocalyptic Winter

★Scarf★

Angry Eagle Anthology

AMY

By D. Stalter

I slid my feet into my fuzzy blue slippers and shuffled to the door that led to the only other room in the cabin. I pushed aside the scarf, which was hung from a brass hook, to reveal a small hole drilled through the door. I pressed my nose against the door and looked through the peephole. All seemed quiet on the other side.

Inserting the key into the lock, I turned the handle and slowly cracked the door open. I peeked through the small gap before I pulled the door wide and stepped into the cabin's main room.

The smell of the woodburning stove mingled with the herbs drying from hooks in the corner. Above the herbs, a newspaper clipping hung in a frame. It was from about ten years ago and showed a mama bear and her cub. They stood next to the same lake that I could see now as I looked out the kitchen window. The headline read, "Bears Spotted in Lee County." I remembered the news story on that. It had been all over the Chicago news for a couple of weeks. Ironic that I was now living exactly where the bears had been. I wondered if they were still around.

Today was the peddler's day. I had a lot of work to do.

I had a little coffee from the peddler's last visit and was looking forward to a cup; once the pot started boiling. I got a fire going in the small stove and set a pot of water on.

Inspecting the bag I'd made from an old pair of jeans last year, I noticed one seam was getting weak. I pulled my meager sewing kit from the shelf beneath the window and quickly repaired the seam.

After my coffee, I dressed in jeans that no longer hugged my curves. They hung from my hips like cheap curtains in a bow window. A bungee cord served as a belt to keep them from falling off my hips.

I opened the cabinet on the far wall and pulled the brown bottles off the shelf marked "Week 6". Fifteen small bottles of tinctures would trade for at least two weeks of supplies. I placed the bottles in my denim bag, then slipped outside to sit on the small porch to wait for the peddler.

It was during moments like these that I felt lonely. As long as I kept busy, I didn't miss my old life much. In my old life I'd been the typical Generation X. I'd been a junior partner in a large law firm. My husband owned his own accounting firm. Our two sons worked with my husband. We'd been a close family.

Until the lights went out.

I'd been home that day. We'd lived in the suburbs of Chicago, far enough out that we still drove past corn fields and horse farms on our way to our offices in the city. I'd taken the day off to plant my garden. I'd heard the police sirens, pausing momentarily to wonder what the commotion was about, but then went back to my planting.

My neighbor had knocked on my back gate just as I leaned back onto my heels. "Sherri, are you back there?" Mandy Bernstein was an attractive retired judge. Her short curly hair was a light shade of purple. She always smelled like lavender.

She and her husband owned an RV and were gone frequently. We had a key to their house so we could check on things while they were gone.

On that terrible day, she let herself into my backyard. She paused to wipe her hands on her thighs. They were filthy—like she'd been rustling around in her attic. Her face was white.

"Sherri," she called. "What are you doing gardening at a time like this?"

I'd frowned and straightened up from my crouch. My back ached from the garden work. I'd placed my hands on my hips and leaned back to stretch my tight muscles.

"A time like what?" I was tired and really wasn't in the mood for mindless chat.

Her eyebrows rose. "You don't know the power is out?"

"No. I've been out here all afternoon. What happened? Squirrel in a transformer?"

"No, honey. Dan Stine stopped by an hour ago and let us know that this was an attack. The entire electrical grid is down. He said to get far away from the city as fast as we can."

"Who is Dan Stine? What kind of attack? We aren't even close to the city."

She shook her head. "Why does that matter? He's a state patrol man who happens to be a friend. He said there were shootings downtown. They'd started just before the power went out. The traffic signals had stopped working, making every person on the street an easy target. 'Like shooting fish in a barrel', he said."

She wrung her slim hands together. "We've cleaned out our kitchen and are packing what we can get in the motorhome. Then we are out of here. We've got room for you if you want to go with us. You need to come with us." Her voice became pleading.

I shook my head. "No. I have to wait for Jim and the boys."

She stared at me for a moment and then nodded.

"I understand," she whispered. "Stay safe. You should start packing now. The violence won't stay in the city. It will be here soon. Pack your stuff and get out before the violence gets here."

Halfway to the gate, she turned back. "Do you have somewhere safe to go? Somewhere away from towns? A friend that lives on a farm or something?"

"My parents are in Iowa. They have a big farm. It's about five hours from here."

She nodded. "You need to move fast. Be ready, as soon as your boys get home." She paused and added. "If they aren't home in an hour, leave a note and just go. They can meet you there if they make it out of the city."

She closed the gate behind herself and I heard her moving through her back yard.

I hurried to the house. It was so quiet without the hum of the appliances. I turned the water on in the sink before I realized that the power was out. I quickly turned the water off. How long would I have running water? I had no idea. I knew the water worked right now, but for how long?

When the power went out on the farm, the water pump quit working. I tried to remember if we still had water when the power went out in town. I think we did. We could still flush toilets even if the power was out for hours. However, I wasn't taking any chances.

I reached for the dish soap and poured a little in my hand, then scrubbed my hands clean before turning the water back on to rinse them.

I went to the pantry and retrieved several empty jugs. Then, removed the lids and lined them up on the counter next to the sink. I didn't need to worry. There was plenty of water to fill every jug on hand. I left them sit on the counter.

I paused to look out the living room window. The Bernstein's were just pulling their motorhome out of the driveway. Mandy caught my eye and raised her hand in a wave.

I stood there at the window, face pressed hard against the glass, looking down the street as far as I could see. There was no sign of Jim's Escalade.

The neighbors on the other side of me were both loading boxes into their car. She was red faced and rushing. He was stone faced and plodding. He shoved an Amazon box into the back seat, spotting me through my window as he turned back toward his house. He paused and stared, then lifted his hand. I lifted mine in return.

I wanted to be ready when Jim and the boys made it home, so I went to the basement and found some empty boxes. I cleaned the kitchen out first. I packed my favorite pots and pans and added almost everything in my silverware drawer. I paused with the silver serving spoon we got for our 25th wedding anniversary last year. It would be ruined if we had to use it on the road. But would probably be stolen if I left it here. I packed it.

I realized that all of my plates and bowls were glass. That wouldn't do. I made a trip to the basement and found the box of camping things. I made another trip to the basement for sleeping bags. They hadn't been used in years and were slightly musty. Oh well, too late to worry about freshening them. I stacked them by the back door.

I checked the front window again. No sign of Jim and the boys. How long had the power been out? At least four hours. It was only an hour's drive into the office. They should be home any time.

My parents lived on a farm in Iowa. About five hours from here. If Jim got home soon, we could be there before midnight. We'd be much safer there.

What else did I need to take? Clothes and

blankets. I opened the linen closet and pulled out pillowcases. These I stuffed with blankets, sheets and towels. I set them by the back door with my boxes of kitchen stuff.

Flashlights! I went through the house and threw every flashlight I could find into a plastic tote. I added all the batteries from the shelf in the pantry. I rushed to the back yard and pulled the six small solar lights from their holders and added them to the tote.

Back in the house, I checked the front window again. Still no sign of Jim. The neighbors across the street were now packing their car as well.

I hurried to the bedroom and pulled the suitcases from the back of the closet. I quickly packed my most comfortable clothes in one. I added several pair of shoes, bypassing the most expensive pairs—packing only sport shoes and hiking boots.

I packed Jim's suitcase the same way. I would do the boys' rooms next.

A crash out front caused me to rush out of the bedroom caroming off the hallway wall.

Jim's battered Escalade rested against the

front porch. The driver's door opened and my youngest son tumbled out of the car, he landed face down on the grass.

By the time I made it out the door, two neighbors were there. Rick Dent stood next to Jim's car. He stared inside, his face a mask of horror.

Mike Garner, from across the street, rushed to my side. He put his arm around me and pressed my face into his shoulder.

"Don't look, Sherri." I felt his body shiver and I pushed him away. What I saw will be etched into my mind until the day I die.

My husband was in the back seat, his arms were wrapped around my oldest son. They both had gunshot wounds. Many of them. The wounds to their heads told me all I needed to know. I felt my legs turn to rubber. Mike pulled me back into his chest and held me tight.

"Jeremy," I whispered. "Is Jeremy okay?"

He moved, still hugging me tight. "Rick," he said. "How's Jeremy?"

I felt him stiffen again. I broke free and ran to the driver's door where Jeremy lay sprawled on the ground. A trickle of blood ran down his cheek. His eyes were open but clouded.

I remember falling and being caught before I hit the ground. I remember my neighbors discussing shovels. The next thing I remember is sitting in a lawn chair in my front yard, watching as my neighbors buried my whole family. My whole life.

Rick's wife, Linda, sat next to me, holding my hand. She brushed my tears from my cheeks and hugged me. "Come on, Sherri. We need to gather some things and get you out of here. The violence won't stay in the city. It will be here too. Where is your car?"

I tried to make sense of what she was saying. I decided I didn't care to make sense of it. "In the garage," I replied.

"Come on," she said, gently tugging my hand. "Let's go pack some things."

"I'm almost packed. I stacked it by the back door." I let her lead me into the house.

"Come on, honey. Let's get everything and get your car packed. Then we can go finish packing our cars. Please, let's hurry."

I stopped in the master bedroom. Maybe I should just stay here with Jim and the boys. Did I really want to run to safety? I could just stay here with them.

"Move it!" The sharpness of her voice brought me out of my stupor. "I mean it, Sherri. There will be time to mourn later. Please, move faster so we can get out of here."

"Go without me." I whispered.

"Get your ass moving!" she demanded.

I stared at her. She glared back. "We aren't leaving you," she put her hands on her hips and leaned toward me. "Move. Your. Ass."

I felt a shiver run down my back and grabbed the handle of my suitcase.

"Wait," I said. "I need my toiletries."

She looked around the room. Her eyes landed on the other suitcase. "Jim's?"

I nodded.

She unzipped it and dumped it. I took it from her and went to the bathroom to pack my toiletries. When I finished, I rolled it back to the bedroom and repacked some of Jim's favorite clothes. Linda watched, but didn't say anything. She took the handle and rolled the suitcase to the kitchen.

The armoire held all my essential oil supplies. I pulled out boxes of amber bottles. I had two cases of one-ounce bottles, three cases of four-ounce bottles and a case of eight-ounce bottles. She carried them to the back door. I pulled the soft cases of essential oils from the shelf and carried them myself.

Linda found an empty tote in the pantry. She lifted frames from the wall and carefully placed them in the tote. Going to the bookshelf, she selected a dozen or so books and added them. She carried the tote to the back door.

I stepped into Jeremy's room. All of his Boy Scout manuals as well as a full set of Foxfire books sat on his shelf. I scooped them into my arms and carried them to the back door. Those went into the tote.

They started loading my stuff into my Lincoln Navigator. I looked at the shelving on the walls.

"I'll probably want my seeds and my planters." I really didn't care whether I had them or not, but it seemed like the right thing to do.

Rick pulled the planters off the shelf and grabbed a shovel and a rake. "Where are your seeds?"

"In the house. I'll get them." I kept them in a dark colored tote on the bottom shelf in my pantry. It stayed pretty cool in there and I'd found that it was the best place to keep my seeds.

I squeezed past the boxes stacked inside the kitchen and entered the pantry. Linda followed me.

"We're going to need some more boxes for this food. You can't leave it here. You'll need it."

"In the basement." I just couldn't get the energy to show more interest in survival.

I bent over to grab the plastic container with all my vegetable and herb seeds when my eye caught the box of vodka in the corner. Four gallons. I would need those to make my tinctures — or get drunk. Either would work for me.

When Linda returned with the empty boxes, she noticed the four gallons of vodka and her eyebrows raised. "You are serious about your vodka, aren't you?"

"I use vodka for making tinctures."

She just nodded and started stacking food into the boxes. When the Navigator was packed, (they'd even taken all my jugs of water and shoved them where they could), Linda took my keys and backed it out of the garage.

"Where are you going?" I'd asked.

"We need to finish packing our stuff and then we'll caravan to Rick's brother's place. It's not too far past Rochelle, less than an hour from here. We should be safe there. You are coming with us."

"But I don't know anyone there. I want to go to my parents in Iowa."

She sighed. "That's fine. You can go on your way after you get a good night's sleep. Or you can stay with us. It'll be your choice in the morning. For now, we need to finish loading and get out of here."

I had spent that first night at Rick's brother's farm. I didn't sleep much, but I passed muster in the morning and they deemed me safe to travel. I'd gotten a million hugs and had to promise that I'd return if I needed to.

I made it to the Mississippi River by eight o'clock in the morning. My parent's farm was only about thirty miles past Clinton, Iowa. But I couldn't cross the bridge. A tangled mess of wrecked cars littered Highway 30. I turned around, planning to go north to the 14th Avenue bridge instead, but a huge crowd blocked my way at a saloon. I didn't even have time to turn around. I just hit reverse and backed up until I was far enough away to turn around. My car started beeping that I had fifty miles to go until I ran out of gas.

I followed Highway 30 back east toward Chicago. I had no choice but to return to Rick's brother's house. I became uncomfortable staying on the highway, so I dropped down to county roads and traveled east. I knew the farm was south of highway 30 and not too far west of Interstate 39. Would I have enough gas to get back?

I had just crossed Highway 26 when the low fuel light started flashing, demanding that I get to a gas station. The sign on the road said that Amboy was five miles ahead. I wondered how big Amboy was. I'd never heard of it, but I sure didn't want to run out of gas in the middle of a town of ugly people.

My hands shook and tears ran down my cheeks as I tried to decide what to do. I did not have enough gas to get back to Rick's brothers. I turned right onto a rough county road. A quarter mile down, I spotted an overgrown driveway. I eased into the driveway and saw the cabin. Behind the cabin was a lake. Both the lake and the cabin were hidden by trees and thick undergrowth.

This had become my home. My fourth week there, I was working on hiding the driveway when I was startled by a horse driven wagon. I screamed and ran.

"Don't be afraid." The man had stopped his horse and stood on the wagon. "I won't hurt you. I've got food and things to trade."

I'd stopped at the word 'food'.

On that first day, he'd explained that he made trips every two weeks and could take orders for eggs and beef and many more things. I'd traded a couple of books for some eggs.

I told him that my husband and sons lived with me. That was my secret.

I'd grown to trust this man and even felt like I knew some of my neighbors through our conversations, but I wasn't quite ready to trust them — even if I was so lonely I often found myself talking to the little pine tree next to the porch.

I'm not sure that little pine tree would be happy if it had understood the promise I'd made to it. The promise that it would be my Christmas tree in a few months.

*****

The tinkling bells brought me out of my memories. I picked up the bag and made my way down the narrow path through the brush and trees that hid my cabin from the road. I got to the road just as the peddler brought his beautiful yellow horse to a stop. The bells mounted on the wagon jingled for a few seconds before becoming quiet.

"Good morning, Mrs. Black." The old man jumped from the wagon and wrapped the reins three times around a hook on the left side of the seat.

"How are your husband and sons?" he asked.

"Great," I replied, glancing at my feet. "The boys are out checking traps and my husband is up in the tree keeping watch."

I wondered if he still believed my ruse. I sometimes felt guilty keeping up the lie, but I felt so much safer if people believed that I wasn't alone out here.

He lifted the door on the side of the wagon, creating a shady spot next to the wooden cart.

Pulling an identical denim bag from a shelf, he handed it to me. "Your empty bottles," he said. "There's one missing. Mrs. Carter dropped one and it shattered. She's very sorry and asked if you would be made whole by a dozen eggs a week for two months. She said that if that wouldn't work for you, that she'd try to come up with whatever you asked."

"That's more than fair," I replied. I watched as he pulled out a shelf and set a basket of eggs on it.

"The basket is yours to keep." He ran his fingers over the handle. "Mrs. Carter's daughter has started basket weaving and there's quite a demand for them. She wanted you to have this whether or not you made the deal."

He leaned back into the cart. "The doctor also wants to make a deal." He set a box on the shelf. Four eight-ounce empty brown bottles nestled in the box. He reached in and my eyes grew wide when he pulled out three large bottles of vodka.

"The deal is," he continued, "he will give you these four bottles and the vodka, in exchange for one bottle each: your migraine, sleeping, immune booster, and your cough tinctures. After you deliver the first four bottles and have paid off this delivery, he will provide you with a half-gallon of homemade moonshine in exchange for the medicine."

"Deal!" I exclaimed. I did a mental jig.

I handed him my denim bag. "Fifteen bottles," I said. "Five each of the migraine, sleeping and immune booster."

"That's thirty credits." He took the bag and set it on an empty shelf.

I spent my thirty credits in no time. I filled my bag with small amounts of sugar, flour, and coffee as well as some pemmican and jerky.

He chatted the whole time I was selecting my supplies. "The town has a crew cutting wood. They have stacked enough wood to get everyone left in town through the winter." He said while placing my supplies in the bag. "They are still cutting and stacking...and will be selling wood within the next week or two if you are interested."

I felt a shiver of relief cross my shoulders. "I would be interested in buying wood. Do you know how much they are asking?"

"No, I don't, but I'm sure they will be happy to make some sort of deal. We don't want to see anyone freeze."

His eyes met mine. Piercing blue eyes that seemed to see right through me. He cleared his throat. "You know, the Anderson's also have a small cottage in town they'd be willing to let you live in. It's got a small greenhouse attached to the kitchen. Mrs. Anderson thinks it would be perfect for you. You'd be a lot safer in town. And could grow your herbs all winter long."

"Who are the Andersons?"

"Well, they own this cabin."

I sucked in a breath and took a step back.

"Don't worry. They don't mind that you

are using it. But they wanted you to know that there would be a place in town that might be more comfortable for you."

I shook my head. "I like it here. But I guess I need to work out some sort of payment to the Andersons."

He held his hand up. "Don't you worry about that."

He handed me my bag.

I stepped back to allow him to close the door to the wagon.

"Hold on just a minute," he said. "I have something else you might be interested in."

He walked around to the back of the wagon and opened a door. Reaching in, he lifted a plastic tote and carried it to me. Nestled in the bottom on a pile of old rags lay a tiny German shepherd puppy. Her grey eyes looked into mine and her tail thumped. My heart melted.

"She's eight weeks old today," the peddler said. "My daughter's collie had a frolic with the neighbor's German shepherd. If you want her, she's yours. Her name is Amy."

He stood watching me. I raised my eyes

to his, not caring if he saw the tears threatening to spill down my cheeks.

"Thank you," I whispered.

"Any time," he whispered back. "Tell your husband in the tree that I said 'howdy'."

He winked and picked up his reins.

About D. Stalter

D. Stalter led a nomadic life in her early years. The daughter of a pipe fitter, her father's jobs moved the family wherever he had work. From dams in South Dakota and Arizona to nuclear power plants in Illinois to taconite mines in northern Minnesota.

She embraced that lifestyle growing up. When she struck out on her own, she dreamed of following her father in his profession, but women still hadn't broken that barrier (yet).

When she heard that the U.S. Army was testing a new program where they would train men and women together to see if women could do the same program that the men did. Dorene said, "Sign me up now!"

She went on to prove that women could excel, finishing in the top ten of her Company. She never did become a pipe fitter, but she did pursue her dreams of writing. These are her stories.

Follow her and find her books!

www.dstalter.com

https://www.facebook.com/ReadAllisonsSecret

https://www.goodreads.com/author/show/18167824.D_Sta lter

OVERWATCH

By Dennis Welton

Wake up Nora!

Nora awoke with a start and looked around in the darkness. "What is it?" she asked, alarmed.

Shsssh. Listen!

She lay very still and listened intently. Above and to her right it sounded as if something was brushing against the wall.

"I'm going to check it out," she whispered.

Stay quiet and be very careful!

"I will. Don't worry."

Nora eased out of the down sleeping bag that was at the center of her nest of blankets and slowly stood up in the darkness. Moving forward tentatively, her outstretched hand contacted the familiar earthen wall that she could see in her mind. Placing both hands against the dirt wall for balance, she stepped up onto the ledge that her toes had located below. Once on the ledge she eased forward until she could feel the edge of the hole. With practiced ease, she silently slipped over the top and belly crawled toward the sound. Navigating by feel, her fingers soon found the masonry wall that she knew was there. She could still hear something moving along just on the other side. She felt her way along the wall until her fingers closed around one of the small wooden plugs that Ian had installed every few feet along the perimeter of the house. He had cleverly drilled out the mortar between the stones that made up the foundation of their home to create a series of peep holes. In each one he had fitted a dowel plug and painted it to look like the surrounding mortar to camouflage the holes, so they blended into the rustic stone foundation. She eased the plug from its fitting and put her eye to it. She could clearly see the area before her in the moonlight. As she looked at what had once been her garden area, a dark mass moved past the opening, blocking her view. For a moment she could not comprehend what she was seeing.

Then, as the object continued to move past her peep hole, she realized she was seeing a mass of hair in the moonlight. The snuffling sound confirmed the identity of her visitor. A black bear! She let out the breath that she hadn't realized that she had been holding in relief.

Nora smiled and had to suppress a giggle at the thought of what would happen if she surprised her visitor by sliding a stick through her peep hole and giving him a poke. She quietly slid the wooden plug back in place. Still on her stomach, she inched backwards until her toes found the edge of the hole. Lowering herself silently back down to the ledge, she whispered, "It's only a curious black bear."

A black bear? Do you know what that means?

"I am too cold and sleepy to think about it right now, Ian. Let's talk about it in the morning," she said, as she burrowed back under the pile of blankets and into her sleeping bag. "You should get some sleep too."

I'm good. I will stand watch and keep an eye on things.

"It seems like you are always on watch and always awake. Don't you ever get tired?"

I can sleep when I am dead.

"That's not funny, Ian!" she snapped.

Okay, okay. I'm sorry. It was just a joke. I didn't mean to upset you.

"Your sense of humor sucks sometimes. Some things you just don't joke about!"

I said I was sorry. Good night, my love. Sleep well.

"Goodnight. I love you," Nora replied, as she snuggled into a comfortable position.

You have to admit, it was a little bit funny.

"Shut up, Ian. Don't push your luck. I need sleep," Nora retorted. She could hear him chuckling as she drifted off.

***

Nora's eyes slowly opened. She always hated having to leave her warm and cozy cocoon of bedding, but nature was calling.

Good morning, sleepy head.

"Morning," she mumbled.

You look like you are bearly awake. Get it? Bear? Bearly awake.

She could hear the smile in his teasing tone of voice and said, "You are so funny I can bearly stand it".

Thank you. Thank you very much. I'll be here all week.

Nora could tell it was sunny outside. The pitch blackness had turned into a lighter hue of black due to light leaking through the tiny cracks and fissures between the stones that supported the house above. That is why the candles were only lit when it was daylight outside. If light could get in from the outside, then it could be spotted from the outside when it was nighttime. Reaching into her pants pocket, she pulled out a disposable butane lighter and struck it. In the dancing light of the flame she saw one of several large serving spoons with their handles embedded most of the way into the dirt wall. Inside of the bowl of each spoon was a small candle which she lit. The spoons made the perfect candle holders and caught any melted wax that dripped from the burning candles. The handle of each of the spoons had pierced a small square of aluminum foil as they had been driven into the dirt wall which served as reflectors. The amount of light the contraptions provided always surprised her each time she lit them.

"I have to pee," Nora said, as she stepped up on the chair height ledge that ran entirely around the bottom of the hole.

So, you are saying that you can bearly hold it?

"Enough with the bear jokes," Nora huffed, as she scrambled out of the hole.

She crawled on her hands and knees to the far corner of the crawl space under the house, where the latrine was located. It wasn't much more than a deep hole with a plywood box over it, but it did the job. She settled herself onto the toilet seat that Ian had salvaged from their guest bathroom above and fitted around the hole in the plywood box. She smiled as she remembered him calling it a splinter preventer. It definitely made it more comfortable for her.

When she was finished, she tossed a plastic cup of garden lime, from the sack located next to her, down the hole. Taking care to not bump her head on the floor joists above, she made her way back to the living area. Crawling on her hands and knees was much easier than duck walking. Looking down into the hole, she gazed at what had been home for the past four months. The bottom of the hole was big enough for two people to lay next to each other comfortably, with plenty of room to spare. A foot and a half above the floor of the hole was a ledge that had been dug out around its perimeter. This was used for sitting and as a step when climbing out. Since the original house's crawl space had been a bit over three feet, the excavation provided plenty of overhead room even when standing on the ledge. They had covered the hole's earthen surfaces with an assortment of carpets, rugs and blankets. With a tarp suspended above the hole by attaching it to the house floor joists overhead, the scene below resembled what she imagined a sheik's tent would look like.

Sliding over the lip of the hole and dropping to the ledge below, she pulled the tarp that served as a ceiling to their shelter back together to keep in what little heat there was. She missed the little electric heater that they had used to heat their underground hideaway for the first couple of months that they were down here. It was Ian's idea to use the crawl space of their home to ride out the winter and wait for spring. He had foreseen what was coming as the epidemic had rapidly spread. People were dying by the thousands daily, and he knew that if they were going to survive then they would have to seclude themselves from others—and become invisible.

"How do you think the kids are doing," Nora asked?

I am sure they are fine. They were healthy and sounded like they had things well in hand the last time we talked to them.

"I know. I just worry about them."

Luckily their sons, Robert and Mason, along with their wives and the grandkids, had made it to what Ian called their bug out location—before the government had mandated that all travel was strictly forbidden. Once the travel ban was in place, anyone caught trying to leave their area or traveling along the roads was shot on sight. The cabin, where the kids were, was located down the river that ran past their home several hundred yards beyond the woods. The proximity to the river had been one of the reasons that they had chosen to build here. The location had seemed perfect at the time. It felt like they were in the country even though all the conveniences of a large town were only a few minutes away.

"I am so glad that you talked me into buying the property down the river and building the cabin. If we hadn't then I don't know what would have happened to our family."

I love that place. There are a lot of happy memories there. Don't worry. They have everything they need. They are smart boys and I am sure they are doing just fine.

The cabin was completely off the grid, had a good well and was fully stocked with food and supplies. By car it was only a few hours away. By river it took several days of paddling to get to it. Every summer the family would launch their little flotilla of canoes and kayaks, making their way down to the cabin. Everyone looked forward to their summer camping adventures on the river. The boys and their families loved spending time at the cabin.

The plan had been to meet them at the family cabin for the Christmas holidays, just as they had done in years past. They had managed to speak with the boys just before the cell phone service had shut down for good. The government locked down the area before she and Ian could leave, and with the troops patrolling the area it was impossible to make it to their retreat. The situation had deteriorated rapidly. It wasn't long before those that had managed to survive the epidemic, or had a natural immunity, begun raiding and killing to survive. The virus had decimated the nation and quite possibly the world, killing millions. Even though the virus appeared to have burned itself out now, the damage was done. With very few left alive to maintain the infrastructure and systems that had previously sustained everyday life, it all came crashing down—and now it was a fight for survival.

Looking down at the pot of water she was heating on the little backpacking stove to make oatmeal, Nora gave thanks for Ian's foresight. He had always been a prepper type even though she had thought it was silly and often gave him a hard time about it. He had always taken it good naturedly and she was glad now that her teasing hadn't stopped him from stocking up on food and supplies over the years.

She reached over and picked up a package of instant oatmeal from one of the many alcoves that Ian had carved into the earth walls around them for storage. As she stirred it into her little pot of boiling water, she thought about how quickly her life had changed. Once the quarantine order was issued, Ian had immediately started work in the crawl space. He built a hidden trap door in the floor that opened downward and was located under the refrigerator. Since the fridge was on wheels, it could be rolled forward to allow for entering and exiting the crawl space below. He had rigged up a way to lock it in place from below once it had been rolled back over their entrance so it could not be easily moved. Then it was just a matter of swinging the trap door back in place and latching it from below.

Looking around, Nora remembered how much work had gone into creating their hiding place. It had taken them almost a week to excavate the large hole to live in and the smaller one to use as a latrine. They had pushed the dirt from their excavation up against the inside of the foundation walls leaving the areas around their peep holes open. This helped to stop the cold winter winds from finding their way inside their sanctuary. After moving everything they needed into the crawl space, Ian had bypassed the electric meter. To anyone snooping around, it would appear that there was no power to the house. He then ran a small power line down to the crawl space which they used to heat the small living area. It worked well until the power went out. This really came as no surprise to them. After all, dead people cannot keep the power plants going. Once they lost electric power, keeping warm was a matter of snuggling up, staying covered and using a tiny heater Ian made from flowerpots and candles to take the edge off from the cold. The little backpacking stove was only used for cooking to conserve fuel. The fact that the hole that they had excavated was below the frost line helped a great deal.

"What were you trying to tell me last night about the bear?" asked Nora quietly.

Talking in a whisper had become a habit. As was moving carefully to avoid making any noise.

Well as you know, bears hibernate through the winter. The fact that one is out of hibernation tells us that it is springtime and things are thawing out.

"It has seemed warmer lately, now that you mention it."

I think it's time to move forward with the next step in our plan, Nora.

"Let me have a good look outside, now that it is daylight."

Nora scrambled over the lip of the hole again and crawled over to the edge of the house. Using the peep holes spaced around the house's foundation, she scanned the sunlit area outside. The snow was almost completely gone, and she could see that it was indeed warming up. She spied an American robin searching for worms among the new shoots of grass that were pushing up from the wet ground. Also, some of the fruit trees that she and Ian had planted looked like they had the beginnings of buds on their branches. Placing her nose next to the hole she breathed in the outside air. There was nothing like the smell of spring air after a hard, cold winter.

Sliding back into the hole she said, "You're right. Things are definitely thawing out."

Good! Tonight's the night then. The moon should be full and provide enough light to navigate through the woods.

"Are you sure? Maybe we should give it another week or two."

The warmer it gets, the more the people that managed to survive through the winter will be moving around and looking for whatever they can find. You know how dangerous they are.

"I guess you're right," Nora said, with resignation in her voice.

Remember the two thugs that broke into the house a couple of months ago? And that was when the temperature was in the teens. Just think how many more will be out and about once it warms up.

"I remember. I was watching out of the peep hole and saw them high tailing it away from the house like their lives depended upon it after running into you upstairs. You certainly put the fear of God into those two," Nora said smiling.

I don't know about the fear of God, but I definitely put the fear of death into them.

Laughing, she said, "That you did."

Is your pack still ready to go?

"Yes. I just need to roll up my sleeping bag and top off my water," she said, as she retrieved two empty bottles from the assortment that was stashed in an upper alcove.

She walked over to what they had

dubbed their water station. Ian had cut the PVC water line that had supplied water to their home once the water mains had lost pressure and rigged the hand bilge pump from his little sailboat onto it. It looked like an oversized bicycle pump only instead of producing pressure when you stroked the handle, it created a vacuum. This made it possible to pull water from the city lines even though there was no longer any pressure in them.

"It's getting harder to pump water this way," she said, as she stroked the pump. "I think the lines are getting empty."

The water came out of the hose in spurts and it was obvious the pump was sucking air also. Once she had enough water in the bucket, she dropped the suction nozzle of her pump water filter into it. She stroked the small handle on the water filter and pumped water through the filter and into the bottles. Even though the water came from the city water system, she knew better than to take the risk, knowing it could be contaminated.

That is yet another reason to move forward with our plan. It will be impossible to stay here once the water runs out. Do you remember where I told you I stashed our canoe?

Apocalyptic Winter

"Yes. It's hidden next to the downed tree where you and I practiced building a survival shelter from branches and debris. I miss those days. I loved snuggling up with you in that tiny little hut. I wonder if it survived the winter wind and snow."

It was still there when I hid the canoe next to it right after the first snow. I am sure that it's in good enough shape to provide shelter for one night. Tonight, there should be enough moonlight to locate it and then hole up inside until daylight.

"Do you think the river is thawed enough to float down to where the kids are?" she asked.

I think so. It is only about a hundred feet from the hiding spot to the river, so dragging the canoe to the water should be no problem. The river never completely freezes. Just the edges and back waters. Those should be thawed by now.

"It will be so good to be back with the kids and grandkids again. I hope they're okay," she said, almost wistfully, as she screwed the tops back onto the full water bottles and stowed them inside her pack.

I'm sure they're fine. The cabin is well

49

stocked and there was plenty of cut and stacked wood to see them through the cold weather. I went over what to do if something like this ever happened with them and they know to stay put and wait.

After double checking her pack, she said, "I think I will try to get some more rest before it's time to go."

Good idea. It is going to be a long night. The best time to go will be after the moon is up. I will stand watch over things while you get some sleep.

"That reminds me of an old song. Isn't there a song called '*Someone to Watch Over Me*'?"

Yep. It's also the name of a movie, I think. I will watch over you, beautiful.

"You always do," Nora said as she stretched out in the nest of blankets and closed her eyes.

***

Time to rise and shine, sleeping beauty.

It seemed as if she had just closed her eyes. "What time is it?" she asked groggily.

Time to go.

Rubbing her eyes, she said, "Ok. Let me make one last trip to the latrine first."

That's a good idea. It will be your last chance to use a toilet with a seat for a while. I will see you upstairs.

Nora scrambled out of the hole and crawled over to the latrine. After taking care of her bodily needs, she grabbed her pack and carbine. Careful to avoid making any noise, she very quietly made her way up through the hole, into the dark house above.

Once out of the hole she pulled the trap door back up in place and latched it. Looking around, she took in the devastation in what had once been her dream kitchen. She and Ian had purposefully ransacked the house to make it look like it had been picked clean. They had hoped that if scavengers did break in, they would not find anything that would make them want to linger or search further.

Make sure you push the refrigerator back over the trap door. There is still a lot of food and supplies down there. You never know when a hidden cache might come in handy later.

As she rolled the refrigerator back over the hidden door to the hide, she caught the scent of the rotting food inside. This too, was part of the plan. If someone searching the house had opened the door looking for food, they would have been met with a rotten and stinking mess. The smell of the rotting meat alone would be enough to send a person running and gagging from the room.

She walked carefully through the house, into the living room. Here also, the room appeared to have been thoroughly ransacked. In the moonlight coming through the window, she looked sadly at what remained of the home she and Ian had raised their family in. The flat screen television lay shattered on the floor surrounded by shards of glass and broken furniture. Trash and debris were scattered everywhere.

"Ian," she whispered.

Here, my love.

She looked toward the front of the room and could see his blond hair in the moonlight, above the back of the old recliner he loved so much. In the corner of the room she spotted what was left of their artificial Christmas tree—

laying on its side in a tangled mess. She made her way over to it, careful to avoid stepping on anything that would make too much noise.

"This old tree has seen a lot of good times here in this place," she said. "I am going to miss being here."

Being with family and the ones you love is what's important, Nora. That tree, our belongings, and even this old house really don't matter in the end. They are just things...and things can be replaced. Stuff is temporary. Love is what endures. The love between you and me. The love we have for our children and our grandchildren. That is indestructible and can withstand any hardship — and the test of time.

Sighing, she whispered, "I know that you're right, but it still makes me sad to see this."

As she started to step away, her foot bumped into a small giftwrapped box hidden beneath the tangle of artificial tree limbs, lights, and shattered ornaments. Bending down she pulled it out and smiled as she remembered what it was.

What do you have there?

As she tore the box open, she replied, "It was going to be a surprise for you for Christmas. I forgot all about it when we moved everything to the crawlspace in such a hurry." She pulled a bright red scarf from the box, turned around and held it up.

"I made this for you myself. Remember the knitting class I took last summer? I worked on this during the day when you were at work. It's the first thing I ever knitted. I used Merino wool so it would be soft and warm. What do you think?"

It's beautiful!

Nora walked over to the recliner and slipped the bright red scarf between the back of the recliner and the head full of blond hair that rested against it.

I can feel the love you put into making it for me. Having it around my neck feels like a hug from you.

"Oh, Ian," she whispered tearfully. "Why did this happen? How did something that we used to take a shot for every year, get so out of control that it wiped out most of the people in the country? Why did the world get so crazy? I just want things to go back to the way they were before!"

I know, honey. I wish things were different too. We just have to play the cards we've been dealt in this life the best we can. Now it's time to go. There's enough moonlight to see how to get to the canoe. Once in the water it is only a few days of paddling to get to the cabin and the kids.

"Maybe it would be better to wait a few more weeks. There are still plenty of supplies and we've been doing fine," Nora said.

We have already discussed this and now is the best time to go. It will only become harder and more dangerous with each passing day. Our kids are waiting and wondering what happened to us. I don't want them to do something stupid like trying to come find us.

"I know," she said. "Are you sure that it's safe to go to them now? I don't want them to get the virus!"

It will be fine. Like most viruses that kill quickly, it burned itself out when it no longer had warm bodies to serve as hosts and carriers. Anyone left alive is immune and no longer contagious.

Walking around to the front of the recliner, she took the ends of the scarf and crossed them over each other to snug them up.

How do I look?

As the tears ran down her cheeks she whispered hoarsely, "Dead, Ian! You look dead! I don't want to leave you like this."

But you must, my love. It's time to go.

Through her tears she gazed down at the corpse sitting in the old recliner, wearing the bright red scarf, and asked, "Am I crazy, Ian? I mean we spent the winter talking like we always have. Are you a ghost, a figment of my imagination or have I gone insane? Are you real?"

Am I real to you, Nora?

Thinking for a moment, she replied, "Yes. Very much so!"

Then does it really matter?

Wiping away the tears she smiled and said, "I guess not. I love you, Ian."

I love you too!

Nora turned and walked over to the front door. She put her hand on the doorknob but before pulling the door open, she looked back and asked, "Can't you come with me, Ian. I am going to miss you so much!"

You know I can't, beautiful. What we had these past months must stay here. It wouldn't be good to have the kids see their mother chatting away with their dead father. Also, it's probably for the best if you don't even mention anything about our past few months together to them.

Nodding she replied, "It will be our little secret. One that I will always cherish."

Besides, I can't leave. I have a job to do here.

"What do you mean? What job?"

The same job that I have had all winter, my dear. I am on overwatch!

"Thank you for watching over me these past months and keeping me safe. You will always be the love of my life. Goodbye, Ian!"

It was my pleasure, beautiful. Goodbye!

She slipped through the door, quietly pulling it shut behind her. After looking around to make sure there were no visible threats, she started walking in the moonlight. Just before she entered the woods, she turned to look at her home one last time. A smile came to her face as she heard the sound of singing faintly over the night sounds.

There's a somebody I'm longin' to see

I hope that he turns out to be

Someone who'll watch over me...

"Goodbye, my love," Nora whispered as she disappeared into the woods.

About Dennis Welton

Dennis Welton grew up on a ranch in rural West Texas. Upon Graduating high school, he joined the Marine Corps and advanced quickly to the rank of Sergeant. After serving for four years, he was honorably discharged and worked as a technical advisor in Latin America for several years. During his life he has held multiple positions in both the construction and the petrochemical industries before starting his own businesses. He has traveled in multiple countries and lived in several states including Alaska. He now resides again in West Texas with his wife Joyce and their rescue horses and donkeys. He is currently semi-retired and spends his time writing, pursuing other creative interests and enjoying the outdoors. He is an avid canoeist, hiker and backpacker. Recently he and his granddaughter hiked the 552-mile Camino de Santiago pilgrim trail across Spain. His current projects include a nonfiction book about their hike and a novel in the post-apocalyptic genre.

Dennis' work can also be seen in Freedom Isn't Free, an anthology that benefits U.S. Veterans.

JOURNEY HOME

By DJ Cooper

Gazing skyward, the cloudless day was crisp and still. Today would be a good day to hunt. I'd planned this trip for months and all Missy had done was complain about the quakes. She should be used to them by now. Old Faithful has been off its schedule for the past year and the quakes are just the parks way of getting it back on track. All the scientists agreed there was nothing to worry about, but not her…. She had to worry about everything.

I had to shake this distraction if I was gonna get the big daddy of trophies this year! The same buck has been taunting me for the past four years; showing himself long enough for me to see him, but never too long. This year would be different. I've been sitting in this bush for the past three hours just waiting. I'd prepared the giant scrub area by planting small pines around it to mask me and my smell. I was ready this year and the anticipation was nearly all that I could handle.

I sat silent in my thoughts, surrounded by the sounds and smells of nature. Waiting. Watching.

I was so focused on the deer trail. I didn't notice the ground had begun to shake. A little at first; barely noticeable. But then, the trees began to sway. I looked up and their tops waved above me in a dance of uncertainty. I watched them, mesmerized by both the beauty and horror. This was a big one, much stronger than the others — and it hadn't stopped.

I'd become so transfixed on the treetops, I never even heard her approach. The terrible growl of a great black bear echoed behind me and I turned to see her. She rose up onto her hind legs. Before I could swing my rifle around, the massive paw landed hard on my left shoulder. It knocked me to the ground, my body landing on top of my rifle. She slammed me again in the back with both paws tearing my jacket, but not getting through the sweater beneath. Then I felt it — her massive bite, sinking deep into the same arm that had felt deadened from the initial blow, the warmth of the blood reminded me it was still there as it erupted inside my sleeve.

In that moment all I could think of was Missy and how she'd begged me not to go. I could not die out here. My family needed me! In a flash of adrenaline, I flailed my arms and punched at her snout, screaming wildly. For a moment she was startled and stepped back. This was it! Do or die! I fumbled with my right arm to raise the gun as she moved in for another assault.

Crack! The pain was extraordinary. As her massive weight fully planted upon my leg, it gave out with a snap; I knew it was broken. The gun was perched with the butt on the ground between my arm and rib cage. I'd only have one chance. Finger on the trigger, one handed, I steadied myself and the gun for her charge. She came at me again; I don't even remember pulling the trigger. We lay together in the dance of death that had ended with a violent bang. I opened my eyes to see the trees had stopped swaying and a light grey snow had begun to fall. I touched it and it wasn't cold at all. This wasn't snow…it was ash.

The next week was a blur. I'd tried to drive out while the ash was still falling strong, but didn't make it far—so the truck was down the road. The bear would not go to waste. I'd skinned it where it sat and had taken as much meat as I could, before other animals could clean up the carcass. I was in no condition to do any of it, yet still managed to drag back the best parts. I couldn't leave yet so I decided to hunker down and wait it out. I reminded myself, 'Missy knows where I am, someone will come soon.'

Day 13

I wish now that I'd gone the minute it'd happened. I'm stuck here because the truck stalled and won't run. My left leg is broken, and while the bone is not coming through the skin, I can feel it. That bear nearly killed me. I haven't heard from or seen anyone since it happened — and all I can think about is Missy and the kids. I don't know how they're doing at home, but the hunting cabin's food will not last much longer. I do still have a quantity of meat from the bear so that'll help. It was ten days ago when I made the decision; while I waited for someone to come looking for me, I may as well keep hunting for the buck I'd been watching for months. He was to be my prized set of antlers this year, but the bear startled me. The buck was long gone in the commotion when the bear reared up at me. I'm not sure if she was protecting cubs, or what caused her to attack, but I was lucky to get out alive. The hide is good for warmth, but it stinks. The stove will run out of wood soon and I can't walk the seventy-five miles home on this leg, so I just pray someone will find me. I decided to start writing it down, because I question if I will ever get home. At least they'll know what happened to me.

Dammit, why didn't I just leave and go home when the rumbling began? I was so selfish in demanding my time to hunt...I never even thought about the fear in Missy's eyes as I drove away. She warned me something was wrong, and I refused to listen.

Day 20

It snowed again last night. I can get around better, but still can't go far on this leg. Managed to get some more wood for the stove. I'm feeling hopeful that things are getting a little better. The snow is a little lighter now; not the dark grey color that was falling when it first happened. Those first snows after were so heavy they crushed the back half of the cabin. I can't get around much and heating with the small stove means I stay in the single room anyway. I hope the insurance company covers the roof. I'm not sure how long it will take to get it fixed with all the damage that must have been done in the whole area. They better damn well cover it. For the price I'm paying for insurance...they should roof it in gold.

Suddenly, I feel sad inside. I don't even know if Missy and the boys are ok. I don't know anything; has she even had the baby yet? I wish I could see our newborn baby daughter. The ultrasounds showed a perfect little face. Tiny hands and feet.... I knew she was due any day but didn't want to miss out on this year's hunt. Thinking back, all I was worried about was how the new baby might take away this year's hunting trip.... I miss them.

Day 23

I heard voices today! I tried to get up and go outside to see who it was, but they faded away too quickly. Hopefully they'll come back. I'm making a sign for the door tonight in case they return. They can see it, and someone will know I'm here. I thought perhaps they were looking for me, but they never even came close, so I guess not. I wonder if anyone is even looking...or has even wondered if I was ok.

Day 31

I haven't heard the voices again but there were some explosions to the west. Big ones. I could see a black plume of smoke rising into the sky. I think it came from the city.

If only this place was on the eastern slope of the ridge; I might be able to glimpse our town. I might be able to tell if it's ok. My leg has healed enough to put a little weight on it. It's bowed from not being set properly which makes it ache when I stand too long. I'll probably never walk right again. I wonder if they even know I am alive. When the truck stalled at the end of the road, I never considered the air filter till now. I wasn't thinking then. I plan to try and hike the two miles back to the truck to see if I can clean the filter, but this leg needs a little more time before I try that.

Day 40

My leg is getting stronger and I've been gathering some things to take to the truck. I plan to leave in a few more days. I spent some time carving on a tree limb that fell through the roof in the back room and made a walking stick that should help the hike. The storms have been bad, and I am not sure if the plows have cleared the road below the truck. If it isn't too deep and I can get it started, the four-wheel drive should get me out.

Day 45

I've decided to wait a few more days. I'm not sure my leg is ready for the hike and I can't afford to be left out in the cold without shelter and heat. The wood is gone now, and I can't reach any more. I started chopping up the Christmas tree that was left from our Christmas outing. The needles are long gone strewn about beneath the tree, it was still decorated. The plan was for me to take it down on this trip, but I couldn't bring myself to take the ornaments off; remembering Missy and the kids. James is the oldest, and when we were all here decorating it, he pulled me aside to tell me a secret. At ten years old, secrets are important. For the first time since it happened, this made me laugh. His big secret was that he wanted a BB gun. He knew Missy had laid the rules out, stating that he had to be twelve. But he wanted me to ask for him...I wonder how he is handling all of this...I should have given him the gun.

Pine burns quickly, the tree won't last long. I need more wood. I gathered some pieces of furniture from the back half of the cabin. I'd found a broken dresser and a few other smaller items in the bedroom that would burn just fine, once the tree wood runs out. I have to begin preparations to leave here or I will freeze and starve.

Day 46

The voices came back but something in them is wrong. I heard a woman screaming and a man's voice yelled for her to shut up. They didn't come close enough to the cabin for me to see them but I'm sure these are not the people I want help from, nor do I want them to know I'm here. I took down the HELP sign on the door. I'd forgotten it was there until now.

Day 47

I'm going to leave tomorrow. The voices were back in the night and they don't sound friendly. There is more than one of them and I've heard some pretty brutal arguing. I have my hunting gear and pack ready. Leaving early.

Day 48

I've been discovered! It must have been the fire that drew them in. They beat on the door last night for at least thirty minutes before leaving; offering more than a few profanities but promising to return.

It's only four in the morning but I am preparing to leave while I still have the cover of darkness. My pack is full of what is left of the bear. I also have my rifle, forty-eight rounds, and some water, along with a few survival items; fire starting material, small first aid kit, snares, a map of the area, my multi tool, and warmth items — including the giant scarf Missy had made by herself.

She was so proud of the new knitting skill she'd learned going to a local lady's group that it just kept getting bigger and bigger. I love it, of course, but at the time had no idea of just how much I would value it in days to come. I grabbed the photos of my family out of the frames. I don't want the people, who will surely come back, to find them. I also wanted them in case it was a longer journey than I'd hoped, and they might give me strength. I brought the small brush Missy uses to sweep up the last of the dirt from the floor, in hopes it will help clear out the filter and any other debris choking out the air in the truck's engine. I don't think I am really all that optimistic about the truck's chances, but I know mine are slim if I stay.

Day 49

I left early, but not a moment too soon. I'd

barely gotten over the hill when they returned. I can't go back, there is only forward now. I watched; crouched under the bear skin, behind a large bolder as they ransacked the cabin and then set fire to it. It is lost, and I'm beginning to think that there won't be any insurance company to fix this…. Dear God, please let the truck start.

Day 51

It took me two days to get to the truck because on the first day I was pinned down until late afternoon, fearful that if I moved that they'd see me. I waited until they'd left before sitting up.

I sit here staring at the truck in shock and just don't know what to do. Someone has utterly destroyed it. The tires are all slashed, the hood open, and wires strewn about. They took everything from inside, even ripping the seats out. The two miles to the truck were hard for me to walk and the nights were so cold. I don't know if I can make it all the way home but can't go back to the cabin. Seventy-five miles is a long way to go. I'm devastated. I need to decide on what to do. I knew this was possible but had pushed that thought into the back of my mind. I will stay in the truck for the night…. Thank God for the bear skin.

Day 52

I woke with resolve. I looked over the map and noted that after the next ridge, the rest of the journey is all downhill. Now all I need to do is remember my winter survival skills training and go for it. I'm both hopeful and fearful for what lay ahead. I heard gun shots in the night. I hope it may have been a hunter, but fear it was more like the ones that torched the cabin. I'll have a good breakfast of bear jerky I'd dried over the fire in the cabin and a can of mixed fruit. I have a few cans of food and eating these first will help lighten the load. Bear has a lot of fat in it, so it is beginning to get a little rancid. Tonight, I'll chance a fire; perhaps if I can and cook it hard, it'll hold up and what I have can sustain me along the journey…. Honey, I'm comin' home.

Day 53

Wow! Day one walking was hard! I pushed myself and made it about halfway up the ridge. Part of me wishes I'd chosen to take the road, but I don't know what, or who, is on the road. Plus, it would be many miles longer to go around the mountain. I decided to head out as the crow flies and hope the compass points true. Once I reach the top, I'll be better able to see where I am and what may lie ahead of me. There is a river between me and home and I'm not sure how I'll ford that yet. I'm going to have a look at where the bridges are and see if I can see them through my scope to consider the crossing. I plan to find a place to stay on top of the ridge. I'd love a fire but fear it will be a beacon in the night.... We will see — when I reach it.

The climb up today was agonizing but I made it to the top. It's too dark to see much of the landscape but I have time to get some shelter set up. I've found a large pine tree where the branches reach the ground. The snow has been deep but the space under the branches is dry and the ground is visible. This will make for good shelter and a wind break, nestled down inside this little pocket. There are also many small dead branches I can use for a fire. My leg is aching bad, and I'm tired, but I think getting some good rest will help.

Day 55

Yesterday, I couldn't move. My leg ached so bad I feared I'd broken it again. It seems to be fine but the strain of trudging through the snow is causing problems. Later in the morning I am going to move forward. I spent my day of rest yesterday creating a splint out of branches and some twine from my pack. I hope adding the extra bracing to the leg will help to keep it more stable for walking.

I've watched the bridges. There are two within sight; one north and one south. Our home is located midway on the other side of the river, more south than north. The south bridge is guarded and has cars positioned across it; but the north one has much the same only in a more chaotic way. The northern bridge, being so close to the large city center feels more dangerous just by its proximity to that. I'll be heading for the south bridge and hope that I can get across.

The past day, I did manage to get the bear fried up hard. There was a lot of grease. I'm saving that although I am not sure why. The pine tree made a fine home for the day and a half I'd spent there, I'll try and find others along the way. I made some pine needle tea; it offers lots of vitamin C. It didn't taste great, but the warm liquid sure did wonders. I keep trying to remember all these small things, as they will help me along the way. I hadn't realized just how much I'd learned in that class.

Day 56

Downhill was sure a lot easier than climbing up the mountain. This won't be that bad. I made it a good distance, keeping the bridge in sight. I found another pine tree and will be making camp under its protective branches. It offers an unobstructed view of the bridge which I plan to watch for a while, to see if I can determine if they are friendly or not. The brace helped my leg and it doesn't ache as much as yesterday. Today also felt warmer and some rays of sun peeked through the grey haze that has been almost constant since it all began. For the first time, since this all started, I feel real hopefulness. A genuine feeling that everything will be ok.

I made a small fire, just for warmth. It illuminated the tree. The icicles flickered like a Christmas tree and I was transported back to the cabin and James' wish for the BB gun. I lay back under the tree, warm and comfortable, my arms up under my head. I kept looking skyward hoping for any glimpse of a star or the moon.... There was none.

Day 57

I glassed the bridge that looked a whole lot closer, even though it was still miles away. It surprised me that the man on the bridge was looking right at me. He had binoculars and stood rigid. Had they seen my Christmas tree in the night? I should have put the tarp up like I'd done before to diffuse the light. That was stupid. I quickly packed my gear and shoved it out from the back side of the tree and crept into the woods. I left a small round plastic magnifying glass behind on that spot in the snowbank where my gun had been resting while I'd watched through the scope — I'd found it in the kid's toys at the cabin. I thought it might come in handy, but this was not what I had in mind. However, if it kept their gaze on that spot, I could get out without any issues. I sure hope they're friendly, but I don't want to give the impression I'm not.

The day went like yesterday with substantial progress down the mountain side. It was time to make camp and I need to be more careful. I am closer to them and perhaps others. Maybe another day or two and I'll reach the bridge. At first, I questioned not taking the road but now I feel good about the choice. It probably cut a good twenty-five miles off the journey and I do believe it was the safer choice. I think I am making between five and eight miles each day. Far better than I'd thought when I first set out. Those first two miles to the truck had gone slow. But as I thought back on the men who'd burned the cabin, I'd been horrified at what I'd seen them do. I don't want to write it down, but many suffered that day.

Day 58

Last night was cold. I wrapped up in the bear skin and opted against a fire for fear of being spotted. I don't feel as rested as I did the other nights. It'll be a slow day.

I made it about three or four miles today, but I'm wiped out. I need to find a place to rest and will settle in early. I searched for a tree to camp under but there weren't any in the area. Eventually I found a small outcropping which had a small covered area with a large bolder in front of it. It was perfect. I quickly cut some pine boughs and placed them inside for insulation against the cold ground. There was a large stand of trees between here and the bridge. I want a fire tonight.

I knew I wanted a fire, I went and cut some extra pine branches and leaned them up between the boulder and the wall, obscuring any light from the fire. I also set some at the opening of the makeshift shelter to block the wind. It is actually toasty in here.... Only a few more days...I hope.

Day 59

I slept well and made some more pine needle tea again this morning. I think it still doesn't taste that great, but it sure felt great. I am hoping to get close to the bridge by nightfall. I'm not willing to just walk up on it but want to look and see if I can hear who these guys are.

It was further than I thought but I made cover before dark. There is still another hour before dark, and I have found another outcropping that is even better cover. There is a small pit inside it with fire remnants inside. I'll use it and have a fire but need to give the location better concealment first. The men are not that far away on this end of the bridge. I can see them clearly and hear some of what is being said. Mostly small talk about families and other day to day things. I think they are military.

I slept a while but was awakened by a loud car engine. The men in the car stopped short of the outpost and jumped from their car. They immediately began to shoot at the men on the bridge. I don't think I can sleep now after having seen that.... I'm so close.

Day 60

I've decided to walk down to the men and see if they will let me cross. I've gathered my pack and tried to make sure I did not look threatening. I'm sure with this limp they won't be intimidated by one gimpy guy.

It took some convincing, but they let me cross over. They need to verify my identity to ensure I live in the area as I'd told them. I'd stupidly lost my wallet in the woods and didn't have any identification. I remembered that my hunting license was in the pocket of my jacket, thank goodness for that or I'd have been swimming.

They put me in a tent and gave me a hot meal of stew and bread. It was good. I'm waiting to hear if they'll let me go home.... I hope Missy and the kids are ok.

Day 61

They let me go home today. I can't believe I made it. All I wanted was to be back with my family, and here I am. They all are fine, and I have a beautiful baby daughter. The sun came out today for a while and it is getting warmer. When I walked in, I startled Missy. Tears welled up in her eyes and she dropped the serving spoon to the floor. I held her for a long time.

It will be a very long time before life goes back to normal, but we are together. As for James' secret? I brought him into the office and closed the door. He looked at me as though he thought he'd done something wrong. I asked him if he'd remembered our secret and he nodded at me, his eyes tearing up. My heart ached for my oldest son. He'd tried to be so brave in my absence. Without a word to him, I walked to the gun safe and opened it. Reaching in I pulled out a Ruger 10/22 semi-automatic rimfire rifle and handed it to him... Merry Christmas son, tomorrow we'll learn to shoot it.

About DJ Cooper

DJ Cooper is a prominent author of the apocalypse with the Dystopia series and other short works. Currently, a student at Southern New Hampshire University to advance her bachelor's degree she now studies for her Master of Fine Arts Degree in Marketing.

She also writes informative articles for magazines such as The Odyssey, Prepper Survival guide, and Prepare Magazine. Her books are post-apocalyptic fiction, focusing on real life scenarios and offering prepper information both within its pages and as a resource.

She currently lives in New England but worked in and around the Cincinnati, Ohio area flipping houses. During that time, she spent much of it in the areas of Kentucky she writes about in the Dystopia books, offering a firsthand view into her locations.

It's been more than a couple of years that she's been known as an internet radio host and the executive producer of the Prepper Podcast Radio Network KPRN-DB, you can hear archived shows at http://www.prepperpodcast.com. Find her and others in the author group. https://www.facebook.com/groups/writtenapocalypse/

Follow her and find her books

https://authoroftheapocalypse.com

https://www.facebook.com/AuthorDJCooper/

https://www.goodreads.com/author/show/6430420.D_J_Cooper

DO NO HARM

By C.A. Moll

The scab had just crusted over. It looked red, but the redness was contained to only the edges around the cut and didn't seem to be spreading. There was no puffiness or seepage of any kind. That was good. It just wouldn't do, dying from an infection from something as simple as a cut on her hand. She opened and closed her hand to see how much it would hurt, how the skin stretched, or if it would crack open and start bleeding. Cuts in the middle of the palm could be tricky. It wasn't bad. It was healing as well as can be expected in this environment. Angie Prescott had been free for about a week now.

The memory of getting cut briefly flashed through Angie's mind. She saw the lid from the open can sliding across the palm of her left hand when she'd tried to keep him from taking it.

She'd stumbled across the unopened can a couple days ago. It was simply laying there in the gutter. She saw it and thought she might be hallucinating because she hadn't eaten anything in three days. She looked around to see where devil number one and devil number two were — or as she referred to them, Dev One and Dev Two. She only used their "special names" in her head. Doing so brought her a sense of control and hope. Using the special names out loud would probably result in, at minimum, a punch to the gut or, at worst, the end of her life.

The Dev's were about twenty-five yards away, near the 7-11 entrance, talking to another man she didn't recognize. The stranger seemed better off than the rest of the folks who're still scrounging out a meager existence in this torn, crazy world. His clothes were cleaner, and he didn't have that gaunt look to his face. The Dev's backs were to her and they were in deep conversation. It was near dusk and overcast. She thought she could get away with sitting on the curb to get the can. She'd have to hide it. She wasn't sure when she'd be able to open it. The Dev's kept a pretty close eye on her. She was really hungry.

Angie took another look around and sat on the curb next to the can. Her right hand slowly reached down and took hold of it. She'd once had a boyfriend named Bernard, or Berney as most people called him. He was into all that survival stuff. Angie had nothing to open the can with. She tried to remember some of the things Berney had taught her. One time she'd lost a bet to Berney. They were organizing the garage together. He said he could open a can of tuna without using a tool of any kind. Angie said no way. They'd made a bet. If Angie won, Berney had to do laundry for a week. If Angie lost, she had to wear whatever outfit Berney picked out for her on their next date. She laughed at the memory. Men and women think so much differently, she thought to herself.

Berney had gotten right down onto his knees, leaning over that can of tuna like he was going to perform CPR on it and started rubbing it in circles on the concrete floor. He had the can open in no time. Angie was amazed! She never would've thought of that. Their next date had been one of the most amazing dates of their entire relationship. She wondered if Berney was still alive. She hoped he was. She started grinding one end of her can in a circular motion on the asphalt.

The noise the can made sounded horrifically loud to her. She knew the Dev's would hear it and come over at any second, but she was so hungry and desperate. She'd steal glances over at them once in a while. A gust of wind would randomly blow by her, stirring up trash and leaves. Was the wind masking the sound or, carrying it towards their dirty ear holes? After some time, she turned the can over. To her surprise three quarters of the lid's edges had been ground away! She pried the lid up and over as far as it would go. Mashed pumpkin! It looked fresh, orange, and fabulous. She saw no signs of spoilage.

She used two filthy fingers from her left hand and dug into the mush. She stuck it in her mouth. Oh my gosh! It was the best damn pumpkin she'd ever tasted. Not the most nutritious thing she could be eating but better than starving to death. Her taste buds exploded with flavor and sent electrical signals to her brain. Visions of Thanksgiving's and Christmases came to her. Oh, what she'd do to be back with her family on Christmas, drinking hot cocoa, sitting around the Christmas tree and singing carols she thought. Thinking of her family made Angie's eyes start to water. Christmas was only about four days away, or so she thought. She'd lost track of time since the great quake and collapse.

Born and raised in Marysville, Washington, Angie Prescott was a small-town girl who'd planned on staying local, meeting her dream guy, getting married, raising a family, and serving her community. Marysville was about 15 miles north of Everett and thirty-five miles north of Seattle. Although it was a small town when she was a child, it had grown from a population of about 15,000 to well over 80,000 in her twenty-five years. Marysville had attracted good families and businesses because of the low crime rate, affordable housing, lower cost of living, and the "not so bad commute" to Seattle.

That all started to change about six years ago. People were leaving Seattle in droves because of the total mismanagement of the once grand city. Residents had to walk around the homeless lying under piles of belongings, used drug needles, trash, and human excrement. The smell of rot and urine covered up the salty ocean breeze when visiting Pike's Place Market. Drivers kept their windows up and doors locked when stopped at intersections for fear of being mugged or carjacked. Small businesses left the city and opened up in other towns because customers were too scared to walk into their shops. Business owners implored the Seattle city council for years to do something about vagrants, drugs, and crime happening right at their store entrances. Their pleas fell on deaf ears.

The city council was more concerned about maintaining power and, more importantly, fighting every policy that came out of the current President's administration. The homeless man raping a female resident in local car dealership bathroom or a mentally ill man who'd been in and out of jail 74 times in the last five years attacking a morning jogger on a pedestrian bridge were typical crimes that went unaddressed. Cops were made impotent by council decree. The Seattle city council literally spent more time, media coverage, and taxpayer money hating the nation's current president than protecting their own constituents.

As Marysville grew so did the population of liberals and democrats. Seattle policies drove the middle-class north. Looking for lower taxes, affordable homes, safer streets, and tolerable commute times, these "Seattleites" brought their ideologies and voting strategies with them. They began to vote for the same policies and politicians that had created the conditions in Seattle but somehow expected Marysville to turn out different. This infusion of voters resulted in the gradual decline of a once peaceful, small town. In the six years leading up to the collapse, crime, drug use, homelessness, and traffic problems skyrocketed. Home prices doubled as did taxes. The drive to Seattle now took nearly three hours instead one. Criminals couldn't be locked up in the town's small jail because there wasn't enough room. Jail was no longer a deterrent for car prowlers, identity thieves, burglars, or other non-violent predators.

Snapping out of her brief reverie Angie wasted no time in getting a second scoop of pumpkin and stuck it in her mouth. She was so engrossed in emptying the contents of the can, she'd temporarily forgotten about her captors. Dev One stepped in front of her. His stench filled her nostrils ruining her pumpkin experience. He snatched the can out of her hand. She reached for it with her left hand and the lid slid across her palm causing her to cry out in pain.

"Well look what we have here, Jerod!", he yelled.

Jarod, or Dev Two, started heading towards them to see what was happening.

"What the hell's goin' on Mikey?" Dev Two said.

Dev One, aka Mikey, had a sneer on his face and said, "Mother's found something and she's tryin' to hoard it all to herself."

Angie was looking down and pressing on her wound to stop the bleeding. If she avoided eye contact things would go better for her. She took out a strip of torn t-shirt from the pocket of her raggedy coat. A black button about the size of a nickel came out with it and fell to the pavement. She quickly picked it up and placed it back into her pocket. The button was the only thing she had left of her treasured teddy bear.

She missed having Teddy during these dark times but knowing the joy and comfort Teddy was providing the little blond girl she'd given it to allowed Angie to be ok without him. The girl she'd come across a couple months ago had appeared to be only four or five years old. She was homeless and dirty. The girl's drug addicted parents were passed out under a tree at the time. Angie spoke kindly to the girl while doing a medical assessment. Other than the runny nose from a small cold and being filthy, she looked in fairly decent health. Angie wondered how the girl was getting fed, while her parents were self-medicating with illegal drugs. She knew the little girl needed Teddy more than she did. As she handed Teddy to the girl Angie had pulled one of the eyes off. The button was loose and about to fall off anyway. When she'd handed Teddy to the girl, her eyes lit up and she smiled.

Despite Angie's cut on her hand and whatever wrath was coming her way, the thought of Teddy made Angie smile. Angie finds comfort in rubbing the button between her thumb and forefinger when it's in her pocket. She would die if she lost it to one of the Dev's. She had to keep the button a secret. The Dev's would take it if they knew.

She tore off a long strip of the t-shirt and wrapped it around her hand. She looked up just in time to see Dev One finishing off the pumpkin. His head was tilted back, and his eyes were closed as he savored the last bite. His "serving spoon" was sticking out of his mouth as he softly moaned, "Mmmmmmm". It was disgusting. Angie thought it was stupid that he called it his serving spoon. It was one of those flimsy, long, red, plastic spoons you get from Dairy Queen. A time when people used to be able to drive up to a window and get a sugar filled treat seemed so long ago. Dev One was as stupid as he was mean.

"Oh man! Yes! Is there any left?" Dev

Two said as he approached. "Yeah. If you wanna lick it outta the can like a horny teenager!" Dev One crassly joked. "You jerk, Mikey! Why didn't you save some for me?!" Dev Two yelled. "Because I'm alpha and your beta." Dev One laughed. "Screw you, Mikey!" Dev Two shouted. Dev Two walked back towards the stranger while forcefully extending his right middle finger towards Dev One.

Dev One suddenly grabbed the top of Angie's head, a fistful of her hair, and lifted. He was six-foot-tall and 190 lbs. Angie was five-foot-six and about 115 lbs. It was no contest. She was forced to stand to avoid clumps of hair being ripped out. She screamed but there was no one else around to hear besides the three men. The streets surrounding the main thoroughfare of Broadway Avenue in the city of Everett had been nearly void of vehicles and people for months. The majority of the population had undergone a purge since the great quake and eventual economic collapse. Trash littered the five lanes. Seagulls squawked in the background in answer to Angie's scream. They were mocking her.

Dev One delivered a punch to her left eye with his fist while simultaneously letting go of her hair. This caused her to fall backward and land solidly on her tailbone. She screamed again, and again a seagull cried out in reply. She instinctively curled up into a fetal position and covered her head with her arms to protect herself from the anticipated beating, but it never came. She opened her eyes and saw him walking away towards the other two men. "Wow", she thought, "They must have something really important to talk about." He threw the can to the side and a seagull instantly swooped down, investigating it. Throughout her life Angie always thought seagulls were cute and sometimes beautiful but now she only viewed them as rats with wings.

Having been a M.A., medical assistant, before the collapse working at Providence Hospital, Angie knew enough about triage to assess herself. She could feel her left eye beginning to swell. She blinked several times while gently pressing the surrounding tissue with the pads of her fingers. Her vision was fine, but she winced at the pressure from her touch. She didn't think anything was broken but it was hard to tell at the moment. She went to stand but felt a surge of sharp pain jolt through her lower back and butt. She felt with her right hand around the affected area. It was tender to the touch and she was probably going to have a nasty bruise and some sore muscles but otherwise she felt it was okay. She was finally able to stand slowly, and with pain, but nothing she was feeling gave her the impression that she had life altering injuries. She stood for a minute — catching her breath.

Angie had always wanted to be a mother but now she hated the word. The way the Dev's referred to her as, "Mother" made her feel disgusting. It filled her with remorse sometimes for helping them and hate for what they made her do. Angie had always been a kind, caring, nurturing person which is why she was drawn to helping and caring for people. Working in the medical field is what she was supposed to do. She had a soothing and welcoming personality. When people interacted with Angie, they just knew they would be alright.

Angie had wanted to be a certified R.N., registered nurse, but the quake/collapse pretty much killed that dream. Her nature and how she cared for people after the quake and collapse is why the Dev's referred to her as "Mother". It was said with malice and sarcasm most of the time. They only stopped her from helping people when it interfered with some crime they were committing.

Although the Dev's were violent and definitely made it clear she did not have the option of leaving, they'd, thankfully, never sexually abused her. They instinctually knew that would be her breaking point. She was useful and that would make her useless. In a way they protected her. They protected her like a commodity. They valued her because of her medical knowledge and the fact that she was a young, fairly attractive, "helpless" looking woman. If one of them got hurt, she would treat them. Two men alone would be heavily scrutinized but two men with a young woman was much less threatening. She'd draw unsuspecting people into their scams or traps.

Angie was ashamed. She felt weak both physically and mentally. Where was her will power? Why was she so afraid to do the right thing? Try to escape? Death. She was afraid of death. Maybe that's why she tried to help people overcome it. Death was an enemy to be destroyed and she had seen so much of it since the great quake. She needed to find her courage. She knew she had it in her. She would escape at the right time.

Angie gingerly started walking over towards the men. It looked like it was going to rain soon, and she wanted to get under the storefront awning. The store was located on the corner of 13th and Broadway. She happened upon the empty pumpkin can that had been tossed aside and picked it up. There was definitely nothing left inside of it. She pushed the lid back down and put it in her pocket. She didn't have a container and if it rained, she could use the can to catch fresh rainwater and drink. As she approached the men, she heard the stranger say, "Yeah. I'm telling you it'll be a piece of cake man." The stranger was a young Native American looking man who had pock marks on his face. Probably acne scars from his teenage years. She'd call him Pocky so she could remember him easily. He wore a trench coat with a black, wide brimmed cowboy hat. Angie thought it looked out of place in the pacific northwest but then again, it was the apocalypse. In the last five months she'd seen people wearing all sorts of clothing that just didn't seem to fit the region or the circumstances.

She was about to sit on an old milk crate but because of her recent injuries she thought better of it. She decided to lean against the large window and listen in on the conversation. It was much darker now. She guessed it was around 5 p.m. Storm clouds were beginning to roll in from the ocean near the port of Everett where the naval base was. She'd never been on the naval base but had driven by it several times. She'd seen large war ships docked there. She'd met a few sailors before the collapse when out with friends or at work but most of them were just trying to bag a local girl. She wasn't interested in that.

"Ok", Dev One said, "but do you know if he's armed?"

Pocky replied, "I've never seen him armed but who knows? I just know with the way things are going for most people, that backpack and bike of his has got to be worth its weight in gold, Mikey."

"Well, I don't think we should chance it." Dev Two said.

"Shut up ya idiot. You wouldn't know what to do with a naked girl in a whorehouse." Dev One replied.

"Would so!" Dev Two yelled like a sullen teenager.

Clearly irritated with his two clients Pocky said, "Look. The deal is I give you the information like, description, potential bounty, and the time and place he's going to be. You guys do the jackin'. We then split the loot three ways and we all get to live another day. It's survival of the fittest out here in case you haven't noticed and it's not like there's any cops to stop us or put us in jail. What's it gonna be?"

Dev One looked down at the ground deeply contemplating while rubbing his dirty, hairy chin. He said, "I don't know man. I only got one bullet for my .38 and if that dude's armed, I'm up shit creek without a paddle."

"No risk, no reward my friend. Besides, that's what an ambush is for. You hole up in a place he can't possible see you and when he comes by, make that one shot count." Pocky was selling it as easy but he knew it wouldn't be.

"You said he goes north on Broadway every night at about four a.m.?" Dev One asked.

Pocky knew he had Mikey now. That's how Pocky had survived all this time. Gather intel and use it to manipulate others into doing the work for him then reap the rewards. He didn't get everything from the jobs he pulled but he got enough without having to put himself at risk most of the time. Cash used to be king but now, information was.

Pocky said, "Yeah dude. This cat mixes it

up sometimes like taking side alleys or going behind or around buildings. He stops and hides for a bit then moves again but his direction is always the same, north. It's darker than shit out at that time. Half the streetlights are out. If you wait in a dark doorway or alley, he won't be able to see into it. He ain't gonna see you, man. He mixes up his times and his routes so you may have to set up the ambush several nights in a row until he comes by you but, eventually he will and BAM!" Pocky slapped his hands together for effect. "That's when you smoke em'."

"I think I know just the place." Dev One said with a smile.

Pocky replied, "You any good with that thing?" pointing at Dev One's pocket.

"Does the Hulk smash?" Dev One said in reference to his favorite Marvel superhero.

"It's settled then?" said Pocky.

"Yeah. We meet here every day just before dark. I'll either have the loot so we can split it up or I give you an update on what I saw or didn't see." Dev One said.

"Ok. Just remember." Pocky said. "I know

where you sleep. Don't screw me over."

Dev One glared at Pocky and shook his head. "I know your reputation. Just be here at dusk."

Angie saw the smile form on Dev One's face. He looked over at Dev Two who also had a tweedle dumb smile showing on his. A shiver went down Angie's spine. She was afraid Dev One was going to force her into somehow luring this unsuspecting, would be victim of theirs into a trap but she'd have to wait and see.

Angie and the Dev's went to an old drug house located in a back alley right behind the AM/PM mini mart to wait. There was a single mom living there that the Dev's offered "protection" to. In exchange, she cooked them meals and allowed them to sleep there once in a while. After getting something completely inadequate to eat she fell asleep on the dingy living room floor.

Hours later Dev Two aggressively shook her awake. Aside from her heart rate jumping through the roof from being roused so roughly, Angie was disappointed. She'd been dreaming of eating at the hospital café. They had such a huge selection of quality food there. It was one of the perks and was convenient since she sometimes worked 24-hour shifts. Angie got up. She looked at the clock on the microwave in the kitchen. It was 3 am. Good grief she thought.

"Why do I have to go with you?" she asked Dev Two.

"Because I said so!" Dev Two scream whispered at her. Angie knew he was lying. She knew it was because Dev One told him to wake her and that she was coming. It wouldn't do to have one of their prized possessions disappear while they were out running an errand.

Angie got her coat on and walked out onto the small porch. The fog from her breath flew through the light of the porch light. She shivered. "Damn it's cold!" There was a drizzle of rain starting and it had a hint of ice to it. "Great." she thought to herself, "I have to walk in this crap."

She walked back in and started looking around the living room. She found a long blue and green scarf hanging from the fireplace mantle. It had the pro-football emblem from the Seahawks on it. She wasn't a football fan, but she didn't care. She'd be warm. She felt a little bad stealing it from her host, but she justified it as payment for all the food she'd helped bring into the house. She wrapped it around her neck a few times then tucked the ends down the front of her coat.

They walked a few blocks north to where the city's second 7-11 was. It sat next to a subway sandwich shop. It had been looted and burned out months ago. In between the two buildings was an alleyway. Dev One told them during the walk there that they would wait in the alley for the target to come by. When they arrived Dev One told Dev Two and Angie to wait in the back of the alley. He told them not to make any fires and to be quiet.

"Dude! He won't be comin' by for another half an hour! I can't wait that long to have a smoke." Dev Two said. Dev Two was constantly looking for cigarettes. He'd even reduced himself to picking them up out of the gutter and lighting up. He was truly addicted.

Dev One suddenly reached over and grabbed Dev Two by the face. He viciously squeezed his cheeks with his right hand, leaned in, and said, "If you so much as smell an unlit cigarette I'm gonna make you wish you'd quit a long time ago."

"Okay man! Jeez! I got it!" Dev Two tried to say between his pursed lips.

It started raining harder and the wind was picking up. At least she'd be in the alley and have some shelter but it was still freezing, Angie thought. The thirty minutes they had to wait was torture. Angie was shivering. She just wanted to get it over with. She was sad that some innocent person was probably going to lose their life, but she felt like she had no choice. Besides, it wasn't her doing the deed. She just had to wait in the back of the alley, right? Angie constantly struggled with the right and wrong of everything she was a party to or witnessed. She wanted to be done. She wanted to go back to her family. They didn't even know if she was alive. She didn't know if they were alive.

Dev Two squatted down and picked up an old used cigarette butt from the ground. He pulled out a lighter. He only needed one puff. He couldn't stand to wait anymore. He took two puffs and then stamped it out.

Dev One saw the man with the bicycle walking. He was about twenty yards away. Dev One had to walk to the other side of the alley to get a good lane of fire. He wanted his shot to count. He smelled cigarette smoke! "Damn you

Jarod!" Dev noticed the man stop and hide behind a tree. "Crap!" Dev One thought. The man must have smelled the smoke. When he was done with this man, he was going to kill Jarod, Dev One said to himself. That idiot is a constant liability.

Dev One patiently waited. Nearly half an hour went by and the man suddenly started moving directly toward him. "He had a gun! Shit!" he thought. There's no way he could outrun the man without getting shot in the back. He raised the silver revolver and gripped it with two hands. He lined the sights up. Ten yards.

He pulled the trigger. The shot was deafening. The man went down onto his back and lay motionless. Dev One was so excited. He ran towards the man ready to start collecting his belongings. He shouted out with glee, "I got me a bike and backpack now! How you like dem' apples, Mother?!"

He approached the man and looked carefully to see if he was breathing. He wasn't. He squatted down and pushed the revolver against the man's leg to see if there was any reaction. Dev One saw the man's right hand flick upwards. "Strange", Dev One thought. Dev One saw a flash and suddenly felt like he got punched in the gut. The last thing Mikey saw before things went black were the dark clouds and the frozen rain as he fell backward.

Angie heard the first gunshot and saw Dev One run out of the alley while hooting and hollering something and her horrible nickname. Dev Two took a couple steps forward, hesitant to break concealment until he knew it was safe. Angie gripped the pumpkin can that was still in her pocket. She struggled with her conscience. If she was going to escape and get back to her family the time was now. If she didn't do what she knew was necessary the Dev's would chase her, find her, and drag her back. She was too valuable. "Do no harm", she thought. "Do what you need to do. Escape. Do no harm. Escape. Escape." She struggled internally.

Out of the dark came more shots and Dev Two took a step back towards her. She looked at the back of his head, his ear, his neck. She knew where to strike. Her medical training taught her that. He was within arm's reach. Her mind argued again, "Do no harm. Escape, escape, escape."

After prying the lid back open on the can she grabbed it firmly in her right hand. It was almost as if someone else was doing it. She wasn't in her own body. She reached out and pressed hard and quick. Using the lid of the can she sliced deep from the front side of his neck to the back on his right. Dev Two screamed out and instinctively reached for his neck. She saw blood squirt out from between his fingers. Angie turned and ran out of the back of the alley and didn't look back. She knew Dev Two would be dead in minutes. "Time to go home", she said to herself.

About C.A. Moll

C.A. Moll is a proud father and grandfather from who has worked in the field of public safety for over 30 years. Born and raised on the west coast, he migrated from southern California to Washington State over 20 years ago. He brings a unique but realistic perspective of what a major disaster or nationwide collapse would look like due to decades of direct observation of human behavior and interactions during moments of crisis. He enjoys hiking, camping, reading, self-sufficiency projects, and prepping. He finds joy in family activities that are both fun and educational in the world of survival.

His first foray into the world of writing, he offers a spectacularly well told tale of the end.

Apocalyptic Winter

ROBBY'S WISH

By A.R. Maloney

"It's time to play the quiet game again." I whispered to Robby. My brother gave a quick nod in response. I opened the door, pausing to listen. It was quiet. The early grey of morning was just peeking over the horizon. We left the dingy garage, moving surreptitiously through the streets of the small town. The soles of our shoes made small squeaks with each step as we trudged through the snow. It had been snowing for almost two days now without stopping. It was cold, but at least the wind wasn't whipping through our coats today. I'd rather have remained in the safety of the small cave we had been calling home, but we were nearly out of food. We needed to scavenge. Hopefully this neighborhood hadn't been picked clean yet.

I looked back, making sure Robby hadn't fallen behind. We had to stay together. No matter what. Robby wouldn't survive on his own. He was almost seventeen years old but lacked any sense of self-preservation. Trying to survive the end of the world as we know it is hard enough without throwing an Asperger's kid with ADHD in the mix.

Overhead the clouds were thick and grey. I hoped the snow would continue falling, dropping the heavy, wet, white flakes. We were both chilled, our shoes and socks had long since soaked through, but the storm would help conceal our footprints. I really wished that summer would just come back. It had been long and dry; water had even become scarce at one point. However, it was easier to deal with the heat than this cold. It was easier to hunt, to hide, to gather plants, wood and water. It was just… not as hard.

It had been several weeks since we had seen any other person. Maybe everyone else is dead by now, I mused. After the gangs, the bombs, and then the sicknesses that followed… maybe there was no one left to hurt each other. I could only hope. But we would still be careful, that was a necessity.

I was used to it being just me and Robby. Mom was always working, and Dad had been gone for years—he had left one day and just never came back. This left me with the difficult chore of raising my brother. For years, I had gotten him up for school, helped him dress. I'd made breakfast each day, feeding us both. I was always there, walking Robby to school in the mornings, and home again in the afternoons. I helped with his homework, on top of finishing my own. And frequently, if I didn't cook dinner, there wouldn't be anything to eat. I was his best friend, his only friend, really. I did love him, but it was tough. Robby looked like the normal boy next door, but his brain was wired differently. He had never developed the social skills necessary to really connect with others. We had tried other groups. It would always start out nice, but then...well...Robby would happen. People didn't understand his lack of filter, or his quirks: how he couldn't recognize or control his loud voice, his random and frequently disjointed thoughts, or the compulsive pacing and muttering under his breath as he daydreamed out loud. This left many people wary of him. I understood the way other people feared things they didn't comprehend. But it didn't make it any easier. It was never too long before we were asked to leave.

Robby had tried various medications over

the years, yet they didn't seem to work. Either they did nothing, or they caused him to feel like a zombie. Having no effect, or too much; nearly robbing him of any bits of his personality. After trying and failing several medications, he finally gave them all up. He'd made the decision to just try to be his best person, without the meds that stole away with his mind. In the end this was for the best, as neither of us could imagine trying to withdraw from the medicines at the same time as the world was falling apart around our ears.

I shook my head, reminding myself that I need to stay in the moment. I gave Robby a thumbs up gesture while shrugging the question, are you ready? Robby nodded again. He was getting better at the quiet game; what was once an old childhood car-ride game now proved to be a very useful survival tool for us both. Additionally, it seemed to give Robby an odd sense of normalcy, which in turn helped to ease my mind.

We crossed the road, passing into a short cul-de-sac which held five houses. Hugging the side of a large two-story colonial style home, we paused and listened. Silence covered the streets like the blanket of white snow which continued to fall. We crept along the exterior of the house until reaching the front door. It was locked. We moved slowly, peering through the windows, trying to see beyond the dusty curtains and into the interior of the home.

Robby began muttering under his breath, his head bobbing forward and back as he spoke softly. "She must have tripped on her shoes. She must have tripped. You have to tie your shoes, so you don't fall and hurt yourself...right, Jessie?"

I moved over to Robby, placing a hand on his shoulder, giving him a gentle squeeze and letting out a slow "Shhhh, let's see." under my breath. I could see a pair of feet poking out from around the kitchen entrance. "Let's try the back door...quietly."

We crept around the house, between the berm and the bushes, peeking through windows as we passed. Making sure nobody else was around. I slipped briefly as I stepped up the stairs of the back porch. I caught myself with the railing. Robbie smirked at me. I glared and flicked him off; this part was always nerve-wracking.

The door gave a soft click as the knob turned easily. Slowly, we entered the kitchen, looking from left to right, listening for any sounds other than the squeak of our soggy shoes on the linoleum floor.

The body, a woman, had been there for a while and the smell of decay burned at my nose. "Pull your scarf up over your nose, Robby, it will help." It would have been much worse, but the cold air helped to tamp down the odor a small bit. A dark, crusted pool of now-dried blood surrounded the body. Her death had not been accidental. I searched around, finding a tablecloth in the dining room and draped it over the body. It would have to do.

Together we searched the cupboards of the kitchen, pantry, bedrooms, and bathrooms. Then we moved to the basement and began searching for anything useful there. Robby had been going through a variety of cardboard boxes when he started muttering again. "First, we find the tree. Then we cut it down. Then we put up the tree. Next, we put the lights on. Then we make the ornaments...."

Walking over to Robby, I bent down and reached my hand into the box at his feet. I pulled out a snow globe and gave it a little shake, watching the winter scene inside the glass: snow falling around a cabin in the woods, a family of bears making a snowman outside, the glowing lights of a Christmas tree and blazing fireplace inside. "That's really pretty, Robby. "

I handed him the snow globe and he held it close to his chest while rocking back and forth on the dusty, cold, poured cement floor of the basement. "How long until Christmas, Jessie?" he continued staring into the box.

"Soon...." Honestly, I wasn't even sure what day it was. It was just winter, and Christmas? Well, that had not even crossed my mind. I drifted, letting memories of past holidays play through my mind. We never had much, there were so many years when the only thing I'd wanted was for us to be together. All of us...Mom, Robby, and me...even Dad. I had never wanted the shiny gadgets or toys. I'd never had time to use them anyway. I'd just wanted a full belly, maybe a good movie, and a bit of happiness. More than that, I had wanted a break, a day where I wasn't the one who had to be responsible. I'd wanted, more than anything, just to be a kid. Shaking my head, I scoffed to myself...sometimes no matter how much things change, they still just stay the same.

I glanced back over to Robby, who now had a reindeer hat on his head and a small stuffed Santa in his hands. He had his back turned to me and was whispering into Santa's ear while occasionally sneaking peeks back towards me.

"Whatcha doin'?" I raised an eyebrow in curiosity.

"Shhhh..." Robby whispered to Santa, "It's a secret, don't tell." I heard his stomach growling and mine started up too.

"What do ya say we look next door?" We had found some first aid supplies, a couple cans of veggies and a box of stale crackers. There were a few rolls of toilet paper, which was like hitting the jackpot, and some girl stuff, an even bigger jackpot for me. After stowing everything (including the snow globe and the Santa) deep in our bags, we left for the next house.

The neighborhood was still silent. The snow still quietly falling, continuing to cover our tracks. The neighboring house was locked up tight, but it didn't appear to have been looted yet. After assuring it was empty, as well as we could, I took a small paving stone and used it to break a bit of glass so I could open the door. There was no dead smell here, only stagnant air. The smell of old cigarettes lingered. I was surprised to see there wasn't the usual thin layer of dust that seemed to cover most every surface of the houses we usually scavenged. The hairs on my arms and neck tingled. Somebody had been here recently.

My jaw fell open as I opened the pantry and saw row upon row of food: beef stew, soups, pasta and spaghetti sauces, rice, beans, peaches and pears, juices, even a couple cases of bottled water on the floor. It wasn't enough to last the winter, but it would certainly help for a couple weeks, maybe more if we were careful. I didn't want to steal from good people, people who were just trying to survive...but then again...it had been quite a while since I'd come across anyone who I could consider to be a good person. And this was a lot of food.

Immediately I began to feel panic rising from deep in my gut. Who was living here? Where are they now? How many are there? Should we take the food? How would we get it all to the cave anyway? Someone else will come, eventually they will find this place too. There was too much to carry, and I was afraid that if we tried to carry it all at the same time...if trouble found us...it would all be lost. Certainly, they would come after us; if they could find us.

I needed to focus but Robby was standing

right behind me, talking to himself. He was hungry now and starting to get louder. I carried a couple cans of mixed fruit to the table and used my can opener to remove the top from one. I pulled a serving spoon from a drawer in the kitchen and handed it to Robby, instructing him to sit and eat. After getting him settled I peeked out the windows. Looking towards the street, I saw nothing. Then I quickly checked each bedroom, all clear. Finally, I turned to find the basement, only to see Robby had already found it and was stepping through the open door. I followed him, the stench of sweat, excrement, and urine filling my nose, and I heard a small whimper.

I flicked my flashlight on and followed Robby down the stairs. Fear threatened to choke me, but I managed to call out a small, "Hello?"

I heard a pained moan in response. Panic gripped me and I found us both rushing down the stairs two steps at a time. When we reached the bottom, I swung the light from one corner to another, finding a young woman tied to a metal pole. She was covered in bruises and welts and not much else.

"Please," her voice was hoarse, "Can you help me out of here?"

I nodded, reaching into my pocket to find my knife, but Robby had beat me to it. His knife was in hand and he was already carefully sawing through the knots which bound the woman.

"Hurry," she implored, "I don't know when he'll be back."

"Who?" I asked, "I haven't seen sign of anyone for days."

"His name is Rodney. He grabbed me a few weeks ago. I've been here ever since. He left a couple days ago. He will hurt you both if he finds you."

We had her free in moments, and helped her to her feet, and up the stairs.

"Do you have clothes? Can you walk?" I was peppering her with questions. "I don't even know your name. I'm Jessie, and this is my brother, Robby."

"Sophie, I'm Sophie." She moved quickly to a bedroom and began pulling out clothing from a backpack which had been shoved into a closet. "At least my bag's still here." I poured water onto a bedsheet so she could clean some of the mess from her body before putting on her clothes and left her to work on packing up.

I had Robby keep an eye on the street while I began stuffing our bags with food.

"We shouldn't leave much of anything for him, if we can." I began separating our find.

I made three piles of things to put into each of our bags. Then I took the remaining items and began noodling over how I could hide them in plain sight. The neighbor's house! It had already been cleared out. If we were lucky, we could hide what we couldn't carry, over there. I prayed, and it seemed God heard me, as the snow began falling faster. The flakes, nearly the size of golf balls.

We managed to get everything to the neighbor's house in two trips. I had a plan. I flipped the couch and used my knife to slice a hole into the retaining fabric on the bottom, inside the frame. Then I began stuffing that hole with a mixture of foods and extra supplies. Not wanting to keep it all in one place, I moved to a bedroom where I slid a mattress off from the box spring and cut a hole into the side facing the wall. I was able to hide several items in there too. I did the same in the next bedroom as well.

Finally, I realized I hadn't eaten either. I

opened two more cans of peaches, one for Sophie, and the other for myself and gorged on the sweet fruit, especially enjoying the sugary juice. My stomach growled and rumbled at the sweetness; it had been quite a while since I had anything like this.

We needed to get out of town, back to the cave, but we needed to be smart about it. I had both Robby and Sophie watching for Rodney's return, while I took a broom and used it to help smooth away the tracks leading from one house to the next. When I was happy with my work I hurried back inside. The continued snowfall would finish the cover up.

Sophie and Robby were talking quietly, and I was happy to see him calm, he was actually engaging in conversation. It was unusual for him, and it brought a brief smile to my face. Even though Robby has a historical lack of any sense of self-preservation, he always has been a fair judge of character. If he's willing to make a connection with someone, I am convinced they are worth the effort of keeping around.

I nodded to myself, I had made my decision. "Sophie, we are gonna need to beat tracks, and quick. Are you able to walk?"

She picked up her bag, nodding and sliding her arms through the straps. Robbie shouldered his as well. It was just a couple blocks to the tree line, and another two miles or so to the cave. "Let's go through the yards. Stick to property lines, fences and brush as much as possible. We will need to sweep the snow back into our tracks while we go. Hopefully, we can sneak out as easily as we came in."

Sophie volunteered to sweep, as Robby needed to stay in the middle and I knew the way back. Fortune was with us as we trudged along. We reached the forest, not seeing any sign of life from the houses we had left behind. Still we maintained silence, having also introduced Sophie to the 'quiet game'. She had given me a sly smile and nod at that.

Almost two hours later we reached the cave which we called home. It was rustic at best, but we had managed to bring a few mattresses, blankets and pillows over the couple months we had called it home. We had crafted a table area and rolled in a few logs for seats. There was even a small bookcase which held a few of our favorites. We had made a windbreak at the entrance, using a mix of woven branches and vines. It kept the strong winds out, as well as hiding it from view. It was deep enough that we had a firepit. It was dank and chilly, but it was cooler in the summer, and warmer in the winter. It felt safe, safer than we had felt in any house since the world had fallen to pieces.

Sophie looked around the cavern-home and gave an appreciative, low whistle. "You two did all this?"

I nodded, "It was actually Robby's idea. He found it, he talked me into it."

Robby, now sitting on his mattress, looked at the ground and began rocking. He wasn't comfortable with praise, not knowing how to respond.

I wouldn't let him off the hook though, I continued, "I don't think we'd still be around if it wasn't for him." Sometimes, in the past, I had felt bitter, resenting him for being the reason I could never have any social life of my own...even though I knew in my heart, it wasn't his fault. Our parents should have been parents. Yet it didn't mean that it hadn't stung. Now? Now I appreciated him. I didn't even want to consider a life without Robby there, with me. I looked at him and smiled. "He doesn't give himself enough credit. He's a good kid."

Sophie sat in silent consideration. Robby

started a fire and I gathered a snow in a couple cook pots to melt, offering her the chance to clean up a bit. We had a sheet strung across near the back of the cave to allow privacy.

After cooking a hearty meal of beef stew with corn and tomatoes mixed in, we settled down to sleep. I offered my mattress to Sophie. Robby and I could sleep head to foot on his bed.

I woke early the next morning, the dim light of dawn barely visible through the hidden mouth of the cave. Sophie was already awake; she had coaxed the fire back and was making a pot of coffee. I closed my eyes and inhaled deeply; my mouth began to water. The aroma…how I had missed coffee.

"Did you get any rest?" I had slept harder than I thought possible, especially with a stranger in our home.

She nodded. "I needed the sleep. I'm feeling pretty good today."

I found myself nodding back. Robby still snored lightly on the mattress, behind me. I found myself not sure what to say next. I didn't want to rush her away. On one hand, it would be great to have another person around. On the other hand, the thought of sending her away, knowing where we lived...well that was just scary. I wasn't sure how to handle the situation.

Sophie looked relaxed, almost comfortable. She took a deep breath and blew it out, then she looked at me. "I've been thinking...before that jerk snatched me up, I was headed north, to a friend's encampment. It's a good twenty-five, maybe thirty miles from here." She poured two cups of coffee, passing one to me. "You two are here alone. It's not good to be alone these days. Perhaps you would consider joining us?"

I realized I had been holding my breath; I blew out softly while trying to form my words. "You know, Robby, he's...well, he's different. It's never really worked out. A lot of people...just can't handle being around him. He's a good kid, but..."

"Stop, Jessie" Sophie had a gentle smile on her face. "I can see you are both good, decent people. You'd like Tim's place. He has a few kids there, a couple extra-special ones too. I think Robby would fit in just fine, you both would."

Robby stirred, hearing his name spoken. I turned and gave him a nudge to sit up. He'd probably heard a good bit of the conversation.

"Robby, honey, what do you say?" I wrapped an arm around him as he sat up. "Should we try it?"

His face said it all. He reached over and began digging into his backpack, finally pulling out both the snow globe, and the small stuffed Santa. "See?" He handed the snow globe to Sophie, then he hugged Santa. "He heard my wish. It is Christmas."

About A.R. Maloney

A.R. Maloney was born in northern Illinois. She has worked as a registered nurse for several years, spending much time focusing on school nursing and children's health. She's been writing short stories and songwriting for her own enjoyment for many years and has recently published her first novel. While she's not writing, she enjoys reading, camping, gardening, music, and running around the countryside with her family. Some nights she can be spotted playing guitar at a local pub.

A.R. Maloney has a Bachelor of Fine Arts, from Saint Louis University, as well as a Bachelor in the Science of Nursing, from Saint Anthony College of Nursing. She has had the opportunity to live in many places in and out of the United States, including Madrid, Spain, where she finished her first degree.

Author of Skye Light: Edict of the Kauri, you can find her on Facebook.

https://www.facebook.com/ali.maloney.5030

Keep your eyes open for more from A.R. Maloney!

FROZEN ZOMBIES

By Albert B. Moss

It was a dark and stormy night, the kind of night that Alison despised. She knew the lightning and thunder would excite the zombies, but, without adequate illumination, she couldn't see to avoid them. Cautiously, she rolled over, and grimaced as one of the boards in the floor under her creaked noisily. Alison pulled the worn green blanket tightly around herself, and shivered. She had always hated winter and hated it even more since the virus outbreak had turned the majority of the population into something quite like the zombies she had read of.

Alison listened carefully, which was about all she could do in the dark, to detect zombies. Electricity had been gone for quite some time. Besides, even if the electricity hadn't been out, she knew better than to turn on a light, since light attracted them. She considered herself fairly well sheltered, given that she was hidden on the second floor of an abandoned house, and had smashed several of the steps in the stairway. Her hope was that the zombies wouldn't be able to make it across the gap in the stairs. Still, she could hear several zombies outside of the house, as they splashed around in the semi-frozen puddles of icy water.

She jerked her head to the side, as her sister moaned in her sleep. Alison wasn't sure whether having Jenny with her was a blessing or a curse. On the one hand, she felt a responsibility to care for her younger sister. On the other hand, she resented the fact that Jenny ate so much of the food that they scavenged. Still, she knew that Jenny was pregnant, and needed all of the food that the pair could find. But, she wondered, how long would any of them last after the baby was born. And, judging by the size of Jenny's swollen abdomen, it wasn't going to be too much longer until that time.

Alison grimaced again, as she thought of Jenny going into labor. She certainly wasn't trained to be assisting in a birth. For things like that, women needed hospitals, doctors, and nurses. But, those things no longer existed. The infected people had clustered at the hospitals, when the outbreak occurred, and the hospitals had become killing zones. And, some of the first fatalities were the doctors and nurses who worked in the hospitals. No, Alison knew better than to take Jenny to a hospital when the magical time arrived.

Still, she knew that birthing a baby in the freezing, filthy upstairs of an abandoned house, which was surrounded by creatures who only wanted to eat you, was not the best idea in the world. That was certainly no place to be bringing a new life into the world. The germs alone would probably kill a newborn baby. And, if the germs didn't kill the baby, the cold temperatures certainly would, assuming that it lasted long enough to freeze. She placed about even odds on a new baby freezing, or making so much noise that it attracted a herd of the ravenous zombies, which would quickly devour such a tasty snack.

A tear rolled down Alison's left cheek, leaving a cold trace as it dripped onto the brown wooden floor. Why, Alison wondered, hadn't Jenny and that boyfriend she had, whatever his name was, waited. After all, she was only sixteen years old. She had her whole life in front of her. But, she had rushed into starting a family at the worst possible time. And, with the death of the boyfriend a month later, at the mouth of a zombie, Alison had to assume responsibility for

Jenny. After all, it wasn't like Alison was an adult; she was only 17 years old herself, and had just graduated from high school seven months ago. Alison snorted as she realized that the zombie virus outbreak had started just as she graduated high school, which was also the same time that Jenny had started down the path of creating a family.

A particularly loud crash from the front yard of the house elicited several loud moans. Alison raised herself to a sitting position, and peered through the shattered window. As the lightning flashed in the distance, she spotted several of the creatures gathered around one which had draped himself across the mailbox. Obviously, zombies weren't very coordinated, but, despite their clumsiness, all it took was one bite from one to doom a person to a fate worse than death.

Alison lowered herself back down to the floor, as she shivered. She wondered how did the zombies keep from freezing. After all, they were dead. The news reports stated that they didn't have a heartbeat, nor did they have blood flowing in their arteries and veins. So, how did they keep from being frozen solid in the winter temperatures? She simply didn't know.

Another flash of lightning illuminated the room, and Alison spotted the tiny Christmas tree, which she had returned with from one of her scavenging trips. She knew that this might be the last Christmas for both her and her sister, and she was determined to make it as wonderful as possible. She smiled at the thought of the silver serving spoon she had found, and wrapped in a section of discarded newspaper, as a gift for Jenny. And, she sniffed as she thought of the brown and black teddy bear she had wrapped similarly for the new baby. However, she realized that she had done such a poor job of wrapping both gifts that the contents probably weren't a secret from Jenny.

Another burst of cold wind blew in through the broken window, and Alison pulled the scarf around her neck a bit tighter. Oh, how she wished she could build a fire to keep them warm. But, she knew that the flickering flames from a fire would attract too much attention. Plus, she didn't have a way to obtain fire-wood. And, besides, her scavenging time was limited, and had to be used to find food in abandoned houses and stores. Hunger was a constant companion to both her and her sister, and it was getting harder to find stashes of food.

Alison considered leaving the small, rural

community they were residing it. After all, it wasn't like they had grown up there. No, they had grown up in a city many miles away. But, cities were the worst possible place to be during the outbreak. The majority of the population of cities had been turned into zombies, and it was almost impossible to keep away from them. Alison had realized that fact early in the outbreak, and had fled from the city with Jenny in tow. Over the next seven months, they had bounced from one small town to another, as the supplies had been exhausted. However, with each move, the trip had become longer and harder. Jenny's stamina had been sapped by the growing baby in her belly. And, as the weather had went from summer, to autumn, to winter, the traveling conditions had deteriorated.

Plus, Alison recognized that there were many hazards while out on the road. Not only were there zombies who roamed the fields, but there were also feral dogs, crazed by hunger, which would readily attack a person. And, there were also highway men who would rob them of their supplies, or who would exploit them in other, more dastardly ways.

Alison knew that she wasn't beautiful. Anyone who had been wandering the wastelands for seven months would be quite frightening in appearance. And, she realized that her body odor had to be just as frightening as her appearance. Still, she realized that appearance and odor didn't matter to the crazed highway men, who would exploit any female they encountered, no matter how repulsive their looks or odor. She rubbed the hunting knife she had strapped to her belt, and silently thanked it for having saved her from several such encounters.

An involuntary shudder passed through Alison as she thought of the three men she had killed with her knife. She was well aware of the Commandment, "Thou shall not kill". But she also remembered how her priest had once told her that that was actually a mistranslation of the original Hebrew text, and that it really should have been translated as "Thou shall not murder". Still, she wondered if what she had done would be classified as murder, or simply self-defense. She considered whether her soul would be damned to Hell for all eternity. Then, she wondered if her soul hadn't already been damned to Hell, and that she was already living in Hell.

She recognized the howl of a feral dog, from somewhere across the road in front of the house. She both feared and pitied the dog. She knew that the former pets had resorted to being wild, and were driven only by hunger. But, in their single-minded pursuit of something to eat, she knew that they would often attack a zombie. And, while she certainly didn't mind seeing a zombie mauled, that usually wouldn't kill a zombie, which didn't feel pain. However, the attack by the feral dog would often attract more zombies, which would surround it, and quickly outnumber it, turning it into the meal instead.

As she thought of the dog attempting to get something to eat, her stomach growled loudly. She reflexively looked toward the window, but there was no response from outside the house. Apparently, the zombies had wandered away in search of the feral dog she had heard earlier. But, the growling in her stomach made her think of how hungry she was, and how little food she had been able to obtain for the past few weeks. She considered carefully whether the two of them should abandon the small rural town they were in and make their way to the next town, in the hopes of finding food more easily.

Alison wondered whether any of the vehicles in the town were operable. Still, she realized that she had not yet learned how to drive. She rationalized that it couldn't be that difficult, since her mom drove all the time, or, as she corrected herself, used to drive all the time, back before she had been killed. Alison wished, though, that she had paid more attention to her mom's driving skills. Of course, she hadn't anticipated that the zombie apocalypse would begin, so she hadn't considered the need as urgent as it had turned out to be.

The sequence of events for driving escaped Alison's mind. She tried to remember what her mom had done. She sat in the driver's seat, and then turned the key. No, there was something about fastening the seat-belt first, and then you inserted the key and turned it. Once the engine started, you released the key. But, she couldn't remember if you turned it the other way, or just let go of it. Then, there was that thing about pulling the black lever on the side of the steering column down. But, what did all of those letters mean? Alison recited them to herself, "PRND21". Which position should she select? Alison shook her head to dispel the thoughts swirling around in her head.

Perhaps she should give up the idea of finding a working car. After all, she didn't know where to look for the keys to any of the cars which might be in the town. Her mom had always kept her keys in her purse, but she wasn't about to try and swipe the purse from the arm of a female zombie. And, she wasn't sure, at all, where the male zombies might keep car keys. Would they be in their pockets? Eww. She wasn't going to stick her hand in the pants pocket of a male zombie.

She glanced over toward Jenny, and, as the lightning flashed again, it illuminated Jenny's distorted body. Alison shook her head as she considered trying to have Jenny walk to the next town. In the condition she was in, she'd be doing well to make it a block before she had to sit down and rest. And, Alison knew that, once they started the trip, they had to finish it as fast as possible. They would have to make it to the next town, and find a secure building to hole up in, before darkness fell. For the zombies were mostly inactive during the day, but came out to feed in the darkness. Alison shivered at the thought of being caught out on the road as darkness fell and the zombies came out of their hiding places.

Alison racked her brain, searching for some other way to transport Jenny to an adjacent town. She wondered if Jenny could ride a bicycle, and then involuntarily giggled quietly as she thought of Jenny perched on a bicycle with her swollen belly. No, she quickly realized, there wouldn't be any way that Jenny could ride a bicycle. Besides, with the weather the way it was, there could be ice on the road, and that would certainly result in a treacherous accident.

She next considered some of the other modes of transportation she had used as a child. Skateboard? No. Roller skates? Definitely no. Horseback riding? Well, sure, if she had a horse, which she didn't. The thought of a pogo stick flashed through Alison's mind, which prompted another quiet giggle, as she envisioned Jenny on such a device. But, no, not only wouldn't that be good for long distance transportation; it might also send Jenny into premature labor.

Alison sat up again, and stared out the window. From distant flashes of lightning, she observed farm fields. That inspired her with another idea. Could she find a farmer's tractor, and use that to transport Jenny? But, she realized that tractors only have one seat, which she'd need to be seated in. Plus, she realized that, having grown up in the city, she had even less of an idea as to how to operate a farm tractor than she did a car.

She pressed her hands against her head, and cursed her uselessness. She had to find a way to transport Jenny, but she was only thinking of useless methods. She wondered if she could find someone still alive in the small town who did know how to drive, and would transport them to a neighboring town. But, she quickly discarded this idea, for a couple of reasons. One reason was that almost no one was still alive. Another reason was that she didn't have anything to pay the person with. The third reason was that everyone she had encountered, since the plague had begun, had only been interested in preserving their own life, and didn't care about anyone else, well, other than to rob or exploit them. She asked herself rhetorically, why couldn't the world be more like it was when she was a little girl?

With that thought, the proverbial light bulb was illuminated above Alison's head. Maybe she could find a child's toy wagon, and add a bunch of padding to it, which Jenny could sit or lay on. Then, she could simply pull the wagon, with Jenny in it, to the next town. Alison was elated. But, then, she wondered where one would find such a wagon. It wasn't like one could go to a department store and buy one. That was doubly true, since no stores were open, nor did Alison have any money.

Alison thought about who might have such a wagon, and realized that families with small children might have one. Then, she gasped as she realized that any small children would have, almost certainly, died in the zombie plague, or, even worse, had been turned into zombies themselves. She shuddered as she considered a small zombie child rushing out of the darkness, chasing her as she pulled their wagon away. Could she kill such a zombie? She gagged as she thought of plunging her knife into a zombie child's head, and realized that she wouldn't be able to do that.

Alison rolled over and quietly cried as she thought of the multitude of small children who had been killed or turned into zombies themselves.

SALVATION

by Albert B. Moss

It was a dark and stormy night, with the cold rain pelting down onto the icy street, as Martha glanced out the window into the darkness of the city. The electricity had only been out for a few hours, but already the temperature in her apartment had plummeted to almost freezing conditions. She wasn't sure what had happened, but whatever it had been had permanently turned off her cell-phone. Trapped in the frigid apartment, she wondered where her roommate Beth was. Beth was normally home shortly after dark, yet it had been dark for several hours already.

Martha fumbled along the counter in the darkened kitchen, until she felt a box of candles intended for use on a birthday cake. Next, she pulled open one of the drawers of a kitchen cabinet, and felt around, until she located a box of kitchen matches. A few inept swipes later, and she had a match lit, which she used to ignite one of the tiny candles. Martha placed the candle on the kitchen table, and felt slightly better with the light it produced.

Nervously, she looked up at the clock on the wall, and was quite disheartened to see that it had stopped at 6:19 PM. She again looked out the window, and wondered where Beth was. It was totally unlike Beth to be so late. She knew that Beth didn't have a social life to speak of, so it wasn't like Beth would be out on an impromptu date. Martha laughed as she remembered that one of the things which had brought the two young women together was their social ineptness. Martha giggled again at the very thought of either of them being out on a date. She knew that neither of them fit the stereotype of a modern, attractive woman. After all, she thought, she was short and round, with straight, shoulder length blonde hair, while Beth was abnormally tall and skinny, with even shorter black hair. Martha reached up and removed her glasses, to clean them, as she thought of the old refrain, "Guys don't make passes at girls who wear glasses".

When Martha replaced the glasses on her face, she noticed movement in the front yard of the apartment complex. At first, she thought that it might have been some type of large wild animal, perhaps one raiding the trash dumpster again. She shivered at the thought that it might even be a bear; some had been spotted in months past, raiding the garbage. She wondered what she would do if the bear tried to break through the door. In a state of panic, she grabbed a large, metal serving spoon, and waved it aggressively. But, then she recognized the shape of Beth, as she slid and stumbled across the icy walk.

Martha rushed to the front door, and pulled it open, just as Beth fumbled with her keys. "Thank goodness you're here!" screamed Martha, as she grabbed Beth's scarf and pulled her into the apartment, before slamming the door noisily. "Why are you so late? I was worried about you."

Beth sighed heavily. "The bus quit running on the way home. I don't know what's wrong with it. But, I had to walk all the way here, from where it stalled. I'm soaked. Can you please turn up the heat, while I get out of these wet clothes?"

Martha shook her head. "The electricity is out. And, the telephones, too. We don't have any heat."

Beth frowned, as she started removing the dripping wet clothing, as she headed toward her bedroom. She dropped her polka-dot scarf on the floor, and, a few feet later, her brown coat went 'plop' as it, too, hit the floor. She kicked off her black shoes, and tugged off her brown socks. Her green blouse only lasted a moment more, before it, too, landed in a soggy heap on the floor. Beth's pants were next, continuing the line of abandoned clothes as she made her way to the bedroom. Her white bra and red panties completed the disrobing as she entered her bedroom, in search of dry clothing. Beth absentmindedly flipped the light switch a few times before she remembered that Martha had stated that the electricity was out.

Martha gathered the discarded clothing, and deposited it in the laundry hamper, before she retrieved another of the tiny candles from the kitchen, and then stepped into Beth's bedroom. She waited patiently as Beth pulled on dry clothing.

"We can't stay here." proclaimed Beth, as she pulled a blue sweater over her head. "It's freezing in here already. Do you know when they'll have the electricity back on?"

Martha shook her head slowly. "No, the

phones are out, too. I hadn't been home very long, when everything just went dark."

"I passed a church a few blocks back that had a sign out front saying that it was a 'warming center', whatever that is. Maybe we could go there to get warm?" questioned Beth.

Martha looked nervously at the bedroom window, and into the darkened city beyond. "I, uh, don't know. It's awfully dark out there. And, well, we're just two young women. It might not be safe."

"Don't you think I know that." huffed Beth. "I've been walking out there for the past hour, in the dark, cold, and rain. And, yeah, I had to run from a couple of guys who were following me."

"Oh, Beth. You...could have been, well, you know...." wheezed Martha, as she trailed off, unable to even mention the disastrous possibilities which could have occurred.

"We'll have to arm ourselves." grunted Beth.

Martha turned and went to the kitchen, where she retrieved the large, metal serving spoon. Beth snorted derisively when she saw

Martha with the spoon.

"It's all I could think of." pleaded Martha. "Can you do any better?"

Beth glanced around the bedroom, before she left and went into the living room. She glanced under the 'Charlie Brown' Christmas tree, which was standing in a corner, and shook her head at the few small packages under the tree. She glanced around at the otherwise barren room, before heading into the kitchen. After obtaining a cast iron skillet, she grunted with satisfaction as she gave the skillet a test swing. "It's not great, but it's better than nothing."

Martha nodded, and then rapidly huffed the candle on the kitchen table out, before it had burned all the way down to the table.

"Hey, what'd you do that for? It's so dark in here that I can't see anything." grumbled Beth.

"Sorry. Those candles don't last long, and I didn't want to burn the table. Here, I'll light another one." replied Martha.

"Don't bother." stated Beth. "Let's get out of this refrigerator that we live in and go find some heat."

"Hang on." commanded Martha. "We need raincoats, or something. Here, put this on." she continued, as she ripped a hole in a large plastic trash bag, and handed it to Beth, before she repeated the procedure on another one, and pulled it over her head.

"We're going to look like geeks!" glowered Beth.

Martha chuckled. "We are geeks. Besides, it's not like we're going to win a beauty contest anyway. Hey, should we invite Angie and Lori to go with us?"

"Uh...I....I don't know." stammered Beth. "Aren't they like, umm, lesbians?"

"Maybe." shrugged Martha. "But, so what if they are. The more of us in a group, the safer we'll be."

Beth frowned in the dim light. "I suppose it's OK, as long as they don't hit on me. Maybe we should invite Rob and Don, too. They're guys, and it might be good to have a couple of guys in the group."

"Eww." grumped Martha. "Don's always hitting on me, and he's kind of creepy. Plus, Rob is so fat that I'm not sure he could walk that far.

Besides, we don't need any guys. We can take care of ourselves."

Beth shrugged. "But, I'll tell you what we ought to take." added Martha, as her stomach growled loudly. "It might be a good idea for us to load up a bag of canned goods. Neither of us has eaten tonight, and, well, I'm getting kind of hungry. I don't know if they'll have any food at the church."

"You and your stomach." laughed Beth. "But, yeah, maybe we ought to take some food. Why don't you load up a couple of bags of food, and I'll get a bag of our clothes, you know, just in case we get stuck there until tomorrow."

A few moments later, the two young ladies rejoined each other near the front door to their apartment.

"Hey, did you put out that candle in the bedroom?" asked Martha.

Beth nodded. "Well, why's it so bright in here?" asked Martha, as she glanced at the illuminated window. "Oh, no! The building across the parking lot is on fire."

"Call the fire department!" yelled Beth.

"We can't. The phones don't work." answered Martha, as she stared at the horror scene unfolding across the parking lot. "Come on, we need to get out of here."

Beth opened the door, and dashed out into the weather. Martha pulled the door closed, and verified that it locked behind her. She then trotted next door to Angie's and Lori's apartment, where she pounded on the door. It was answered only a moment later by Angie.

Martha explained that they were going to the church that Beth had seen on the way home. She invited Angie and Lori to join them. After a quick discussion, both Angie and Lori left their apartment together.

"Hey, girls, where are you going?" called a male voice from the shadows.

Beth grimaced, as she whispered, "Crap! It's your secret admirer, Don. And, I think that's Rob with him."

Martha frowned, "We're heading down to the church to get warm. Would you two like to walk with us?"

Beth whispered urgently, "Martha! Why'd you invite them along?".

Don chuckled. "Sure would enjoy a night out with some beautiful ladies. Hey, Rob, maybe we'll get lucky."

"The only way you'll get lucky, you pig, is if you find a dog in heat." growled Beth, as she stalked down the sidewalk.

Martha hurried to keep up and was followed by Angie and Lori. Rob and Don followed a discrete distance behind the ladies.

The first two blocks were uneventful, although everyone became aware of a number of houses and apartments on fire throughout the city. The thick black smoke hung heavily in the rainy air. They observed many vehicles scattered haphazardly in the street, left where they had stalled by their drivers.

"I wish I knew what did this." stated Martha.

Don spoke up. "I think it was the Iranians. I've never trusted them anyway."

"No, no." corrected Rob. "I think it was the North Koreans."

"Could have been the Chinese." added

Angie.

"Yeah, but why would they attack Stevensonville?" asked Martha. "I mean, we're just a small, unimportant town. What would they gain by attacking this small town?"

"Maybe they didn't just attack this small town." volunteered Angie. "I'll bet it was one of those EMP weapons."

"EMP weapon?" asked Martha. "But, why would they use one against Stevensonville?"

"It wouldn't be just against Stevensonville." corrected Angie. "It would be against the whole country."

"What?" gasped Martha. "You mean, the whole country is blacked out?"

"Probably so." stated Angie.

"Well, how long will it take them to fix it?" asked Martha, with a voice which cracked.

"Probably a couple of years." sighed Angie.

"Years?" screamed Martha. "What about my parents? What about my sisters?"

"They'll be in the dark and on their own." answered Angie. "There's nothing any of us can do to help them. We're going to have our hands full just keeping ourselves alive."

Tears started running down Martha's face, as Beth slipped her arm around her shoulders. "We'll take care of each other."

Don looked over at Rob. "Crap. Two strikes."

Rob shrugged. "Maybe there'll be some single girls at the church?"

The group walked on in silence for the next couple of blocks. Martha had hoped that they could make it to the church without encountering anyone else, but her hopes were dashed when two men stepped out from behind a parked truck.

"Hey, cuz, look what we have here, a bunch of fine-looking ladies in need of some serious lovin." laughed one of the men.

"Which one do you want?" laughed the other guy.

"You know me. I like some meat on my

bones. I'll take the short round one. You can have your pick of the others." laughed the first guy.

"We're really not interested." stated Martha, as she edged sideways away from the guys.

"You don't have choice." stated the first guy, with an edge to his voice. "Now, get ready for some serious lovin, and gimme a kiss."

As the first guy stepped closer to Martha, she swung the large, metal serving spoon, which bashed into his nose.

"Ow! What'd you do that for, you stupid idiot. Now I'm going to have to cut you." growled the first guy as he pulled a switchblade knife from his pocket.

Martha stepped back and readied the serving spoon for another swing. As everyone was watching Martha and the first guy, Beth stepped forward as she swung the cast iron skillet. '<BONG>' The first guy collapsed into a heap.

"Hey, what'd you do to my cousin?" yelled the second guy. Both Martha and Beth readied their improvised weapons.

"Whoa. No, I don't want no trouble. You can go. Just let me get my cousin out of here. Please." stammered the second guy.

Martha and Beth went around the two guys and were closely followed by the rest of their group. They maintained a rapid pace for the next few blocks, before anyone spoke.

"Did you kill him?" asked Angie.

"I..I..I...don't know." stuttered Beth. "I hit him pretty hard. But, he was going to hurt my friend."

"Well, you did good." smiled Angie.

"Uh, thanks, I think." replied Beth.

"Hey, us gals ought to stick together." stated Angie, as Don snickered. "No, I don't mean like that. I mean, well, we can take care of each other. And, there's safety in numbers. So, what do you think? Want to pal around with us?"

Beth looked questioningly at Martha.

"I suppose it wouldn't hurt. I mean, well, you know, we're not, umm, I mean, well, like..." stammered Martha.

"It's OK. We understand. It'll be strictly platonic. I'm just thinking that, well, at night, it might be good to have a couple of people to stand watch, just so that someone doesn't try to steal our stuff." explained Angie.

It was only a few minutes later that the group arrived at the church. They made their introductions, and were pointed toward a corner of the nave, where the four ladies had a seat on the floor, while the two guys wandered away. Martha studied the architecture of the church, and realized that the heat was being provided by a small wood-stove behind the alter.

Martha watched as the minister added a few sticks of wood to the small, black wood-stove, before he stirred a large metal pot, which was resting on top of the stove. Reluctantly, she examined the contents of the bag of cans she'd brought, and selected four cans, which she carried up to the minister. She volunteered the cans to the minister, who gladly accepted them. It required only a few moments before he had them opened and added to the soup on top of the stove.

"Bless you, my child. I knew that the Lord would provide us with food on this horrible evening." stated the minister.

"It's the least that we can do." replied Martha. "Do you know what happened? Why are the electricity and the telephones out?"

"I do not know, but, surely, it is the work of the Devil. But, the faithful will survive and grow stronger." answered the minister.

Martha smiled and nodded, although she really didn't believe the minister. Still, she had shelter. And, at least for the coming night, she had food and water. Plus, she had an improvised weapon. But, she considered her most important asset was the fact that she was with her friends.

About Albert B. Moss

Mr. Moss lives on a small farm in the foothills of the Appalachian Mountains, in northeastern Kentucky, with his devoted horse, who he rescued from a kill-pen, three days before it was due to be sent to slaughter. When he's not working on the farm, or writing post-apocalyptic stories, he works, remotely, for a large multi-national company as a cryptographer. His degrees are in electrical engineering, although he has 15 years of experience as a computer programmer, and 20 years of experience as a cryptographer.

NEVER TOO OLD

By Christi Reed

I sat as close as I could get, next to the wood stove, desperately trying to absorb some of the heat. I knew that there was very little chance that I would survive until spring. In fact, it was hard to believe that I had made it this long without being killed.

I thought back on what had happened because even that was better than thinking about how very cold, I was. When the power suddenly went out, the world had gone totally crazy. People who had been friends and neighbors, suddenly became predators. I knew the only way to survive was to get as far away from any other people as I could.

I found an old backpack that one of the kids had left behind when they moved out. I shoved all the food I could into it. I filled it with bags of rice, dried beans, baking mix, and anything else I could fit in it. I knew it was going to be heavy, probably more weight than I had carried in the last 10 years, but I couldn't waste any food. There were still canned goods and bottled water. I needed to find another way to carry the rest. In the attic I found one of those suitcases with wheels on them so you could pull them. I managed to pack most of the rest of the food into it and waited for darkness. There was no room to pack clothing in the bags, so I put on everything I could layering it one thing on top of another.

When it was dark enough to hide, I snuck out of the town. I had a destination in mind. When we were kids, playing in the woods, we had found what we called our Secret Play House. It had to have capitals because it was so cool.

It had taken me all night to reach it. It never seemed like it was that far away from the house when we were kids. When I finally saw it in the early morning light, I was amazed at how good our childish imaginations had been. Our Secret Play House looked a lot more like a falling down sap shack to me.

As bad as it looked, it was still some shelter from the elements. I poked my head inside and saw that the small wood stove was still there where I remembered it. Putting the bags inside I curled up on the hard, dirty boards of the floor and slept. For weeks I gathered fallen branches to use for firewood. I used mud and moss to plug as many holes in the walls as I could. There were still leeks in the woods and a few black berries still on the bushes. I found some walnuts and acorns that the squirrels had missed. I gathered what I could, every little bit I found was important.

I thought about trying to make it back into town to try and find more food or bedding, but I wasn't sure that I could make it there and back. The arthritis in my knee and hips had made the trip out here torture. I didn't think I could force myself to do it twice. When the weather got colder, I piled fallen leaves and moss in the corner for a bed and covered up with a knitted scarf. It didn't offer much warmth, but every little bit helped. Getting old had been hard enough before the end of the world, now it was it was pretty much a death sentence. More than once I wished that I could just hibernate through the winter like a bear. Sleeping through the cold winter months to awaken in the spring sounded like a great idea.

It was peaceful all alone in the woods, but lonely. I had never been much of a people person, but I really missed my books. My mind sometimes wandered, and I would find myself remembering some of the stories I had read. I hoped that my children had found somewhere safe, but there was no way to check on them. I wondered sometimes if dying would be such a bad thing. This survival stuff seemed like it was something for younger people to try. I remember reading somewhere that freezing to death was a peaceful way to go. You just got cold and fell asleep and never woke up. Still, I wasn't quite ready to give up yet.

I lost track of the months. At first, I had tried to track time by making marks on the walls with a rock for each day. After a while it just didn't seem all that important. Once in my dreams I thought I heard bells and people talking, but I knew it had to be a dream. I didn't used to remember my dreams, but it seemed like lately dreams were all I had, and they were much better than this reality.

I woke, or thought I did, to warmth and the sound of people talking. Someone held a warm cup to my lips. Tea! It had been so long since I had tasted tea, and it was sweet! I slowly sipped from the cup as I fought to open my eyes.

I was sure that I was still dreaming and didn't really want to wake up.

"Drink just a little more, you need the liquid. We were almost too late in finding you." A voice I'd never heard before said. I felt myself being lifted and propped up so that I was almost sitting. I was on something soft and my hip didn't hurt like it did most mornings in the cold.

"Where am I? Who are you? Am I still dreaming?" I had to know if I was finally losing my mind.

"Easy, it's ok, you're safe here." A deep voice tried to soothe me. "We have been looking for people who ran like you did. We are banding together to try and get through this."

I finally got my eyes open enough to see that I was in a log cabin lit with candles. There was what looked like a huge fire in a fireplace. As my eyes moved past the fireplace to the other side of the room, I couldn't believe my eyes. "Is that a Christmas tree?"

For some reason this made everyone laugh. One young woman answered me, "Yes, you're not dreaming or crazy. We think its December now, so we wanted to try and keep some of the traditions for our kids. We don't have fancy lights or presents but that's not really what Christmas started out as anyway. We're just celebrating having made it this long."

"How long has it been? I've lost track of so much time being all alone." I still wasn't really sure if any of this was real.

"We think it's been about 5 months since the lights went out. It's only in the last few weeks that things have started to settle down." A young man answered as he put his arm around the woman I'd been talking to. "I'm sorry it took us so long to find you, but it really wasn't safe before now to try looking."

"You have nothing to be sorry for. Thank you very much for taking a chance looking at all. Is there anything I can do to help here?" I really didn't like to feel useless after having to do everything by myself.

"You don't by any chance know how to fix a turkey do you? We managed to kill one earlier but none of us really know how to get the feathers off it. We've been living off the food we had stored and salvaged from deserted houses. None of us are very good with hunting and cooking." The young lady asked.

"As a matter of fact, I do know how. We

will need a big pot of boiling water to scald the bird before we pluck it." Imagine that! There were some things that older people could help with. Maybe there was a place for me in this world of survival after all.

As everyone sat eating turkey and rice that evening, I thought back to all the holiday meals of the past. The wooden serving spoon would have been a sterling silver serving spoon at those meals, but the wooden one worked just as well, and looked like it was hand carved.

I spent a lot of time that winter teaching the youngsters how to prepare food, cut up game, and how to knit and sew. It felt almost like having my own children back again. Even though we were getting low on food, I made them save some of the potatoes for seed in the spring. When they went out on salvage trips, I asked them to look for canning jars and the lids for them. They had seen them but didn't know how to use them.

In the evenings after dinner we would all sit and talk about what they needed, and what needed to be done in the spring. For the first time since the power died, I found that I was looking forward to the spring. For now, we were busy planning. Hopefully we could find the seeds we would need for a garden in the spring.

The days were finally getting a bit warmer. We were getting more sun and fewer storms. We had sent the men out to hunt. Warmer weather, while good for all of us, meant that it would be harder to keep meat from spoiling. We women were trying to get the inside of the cabin cleaned and organized as much as possible. It was the closest we could get to spring cleaning, perhaps. When one of the kids outside let out a yell, we were smart enough not to go running out the door.

Looking out the window, we saw 5 scruffy looking men standing in the yard. While not fat by any means, these five also didn't look like they had missed many meals. Considering how hard food was to find in this new reality, that meant that they could only be raiders. We knew we didn't have long before they tried entering the cabin.

"Ladies, this is what we will do." I quickly laid out a plan. I truly hoped that none of our group would end up being injured. We couldn't just aim at driving them off, because raiders would just keep coming back.

"Come out of there!" The leader yelled.

"If you don't come out, we will kill this boy and then come in after you."

"You can't get us all before the men get back here." I yelled back.

"We know your men are gone. We watched them leave this morning. All we want is you women and the food." He said that as if it wasn't a death sentence.

My job was to distract him and try to get the boy away. Jerry was a good kid and I wasn't willing to let him die for the rest of us. I stepped out onto the porch, making sure to keep the pistol in my hand hidden in the folds of my clothing. That was easier than it would have been a few months ago. My clothing hung on me now only held up by the string I used for a belt.

I knew that I had to get closer to them. I wasn't a very good shot with the pistol. I walked down the steps and moved toward them.

"That's far enough, granny! You're not the women we are after." The leader said with a leer.

I took another step and pretended to stumble, bringing the pistol up and shot for his chest. I didn't wait to see if I had actually hit him. I grabbed Jerry and fell to the ground. As I did all the women inside shoved rifle barrels out the windows and shot towards the men.

We used a lot more bullets than we probably should have, but none of us were used to using the guns. When the shooting stopped and we had time to look around, we counted four of the raiders on the ground. One had gotten away. We were all still in shock over what we had done, when we heard clapping.

Looking toward the sound, we saw two men with rifles slung on their backs at the edge of the trees. It took some time to realize that they also had the other raider on the ground.

"Good job! We've been tracking this bunch for a couple days. They raided another house a couple of miles from here." One of the men said. "If you don't mind, we'll take this one with us. We need to find where their base is and see if the women they took are still alive."

"Please take him! If the women need help, we would be glad to do what we can." Sherry spoke up. "Our men should be back soon, and they can help clean up this mess."

"You did the right thing. It is hard to take a life, but we are basically reduced to old west rules at the moment. It's kill or be killed out there. Hopefully, it will get to the point where we can form communities again." One of the men reassured us before they left.

We were all still sitting on the porch staring at the dead bodies when the men got back from hunting. None of us could stand the idea of touching the bodies. We were still trying to deal with the idea that we had killed other human beings.

The men took care of stripping the bodies and dug holes to bury them. Everyone was quiet that night. Each of us was thinking about how the world had changed. It was slowly getting better. However, as that day had shown we still needed to be cautious. As the days passed, we also remembered that there were other good people out there, just like us they were trying to survive.

As the weather continued to warm, we filled all the empty cans we had saved and filled them with dirt. It was time to try starting some of the seeds they had salvaged. If we could get them started inside, we had a better chance of a healthy garden this summer. Spring had always been a sign of new beginnings for me. It stood for a time of rebirth and new growth.

We were all outside trying to clear and dig up an area to use for a garden when our next visitors appeared. At first, we didn't recognize them. They were no longer bundled up in winter gear.

"Hello, the cabin." They called from the edge of the tree line. "We were out this way and thought we'd see how you were doing."

"Hello, nice to see friendly faces after all this time." Sherry called out as she realized that these were the two men who had taken the last raider away. "Did you find the women you were looking for?"

"We did. They had been abused and were in bad shape, but we think they will be ok. They are back with their families now." One of the men answered. "Looks like you're working hard, need any help?"

"We're just trying to get the ground ready for a garden. We really don't know very much about how to go about it though. Well, granny does, but the rest of us are pretty clueless." Seth replied. "We mostly lived in town before the power died."

"We can give you a hand with that. Do you have seeds to plant? My name is Mark and this guy is Tom." he said, gesturing to his companion.

"We have some seeds that we salvaged from empty houses. Not sure if it's enough or a good variety. Some things we have a lot of if you need some." Sam offered.

Mark looked over, "We could trade some work on your garden for the extra seeds that you don't need, if that sounds fair to you?

Sam grinned, "Not sure about that, sounds like we are getting the best part of that deal."

The men took over the heavy digging while the kids got in the way trying to help. At least that was the excuse they gave for playing in the dirt. We, being smart women, sat back and listened to them chat while they worked. At one point where they mentioned trips into town, I spoke up. "If you see canning jars and lids on your trips, we could use more of them. Canning vegetables and extra meat would be easier than trying to dry all of it."

Mark nodded, "We'll see what we can find. We could trade canning lessons for the jars if we find them."

"We can do that even if you don't find any more jars. I would be happy to pass on some of the knowledge I have. You know at one point this winter I almost gave up and let myself die because I couldn't see how an old lady like me could be of any use in this new world." I commented. "It seems like a miracle to me that there is something I can do to make life better now."

About Christi Reed

Christi Reed grew up helping her mother and grandmother garden and can. She can still remember all the hours of prepping vegetables to be canned. When her grandmother died, they stopped doing as much gardening, but those early memories stayed with her.

She's always loved to read and tried a couple of times to write but never had the confidence to do anything with it. She's 62 years old now and retired and decided to give writing a try again. Maybe this time, she hopes, she will have better luck.

GABRIEL

By Susan Isenberg

Chapter 1

Ell rolled over on her back, staring into the darkness, panicked. Her throat felt raw from the effort of drawing enough air into her lungs. Her hair and clothes were plastered to her skin with perspiration, and she wept. After all her tears were spent, she made her way through the darkened room to the bathroom, having memorized the layout from countless episodes in the past two years. She stared at her reflection in the mirror. The woman staring back at her with swollen red-rimmed eyes, knotted and tangled waist-length hair, had a worried expression furrowing her brow. Moving closer, she studied herself, tilting her chin slightly from left to right, examining her face. She squinted at the woman she had become; strong, lean, and distrustful. Never again would a man rule over her or hurt her, she thought as she traced the three-inch scar over her left eye. Her grandfather's steely aquamarine eyes stared back at her, guarded, with unblinking resolve. Shaking off the uneasy feeling, she raked her fingers through her hair, pulled it back into a loose floppy twist secured with a clip. I'll brush and braid it later. Sadie and Griffin will love me regardless, she thought, with a slight lift to the corners of her heart-shaped lips. Coffee time.

In the kitchen, while waiting for water to boil, she added fresh ground coffee to the French press. Sadie and Griffin, her Neapolitan mastiffs, greeted her with soft nudges against her thighs. Ell obliged with a hug for each of them, then washed the drool from her cheeks. As the water heated, she walked to the window, pushed the curtain aside to watch the sunrise above the eastern horizon, brighten from gray to salmon. Although the winters in central Alabama were usually not extreme, firewood was always a necessity for warmth. Winter will be here soon, she thought, as she watched brown and yellow leaves floating lazily to the forest floor.

Soon it will be Christmas; I used to love decorating Christmas trees, she thought. Shoving the depressing thoughts aside, she stepped away from the window, wondering what catastrophe today would bring. Silently she prayed, "God, take my fear upon your shoulders, guide me through this day with courage and sound judgment." After pouring a mug of coffee, she called out, "Come on you two, let's go hunting. Time to stock up on meat for winter. Lord knows it takes a ton for you two." Two sets of green eyes appeared around the kitchen island, butts wagging, slobber dripping on the floor. Ell laughed at the duo. "Go get your harnesses while I get dressed," she told them. Obediently they loped down the hall, their loose blue-gray coats rippling in waves. The only sound in the house was the ticking of their nails on the tiled floor.

Ell pulled on a pair hunting pants, tank top, a dark tan long sleeve shirt, along with wool socks. It was a mild November day. She pulled on waterproof snake boots. Since they were headed toward the creek at the back of her property, it might be a good idea. After harnessing the dogs, she pulled out the game cart, loaded it with her backpack, crossbow, quiver, and a tarp. After winding her long braid under the cap, she strapped a knife at her waist, pulled the slide of her XD.40 pistol to verify it was loaded. She placed a spare magazine in her left cargo pocket. Pulling the door shut, she locked it.

Once outside, the mastiffs blocked her path as they sniffed the ground in a zigzag pattern, looked at her, and then headed down the hill. When Ell arrived at the bottom of the hill, she could see Griffin standing over a body with one paw on its back. From 100 yards away, she couldn't tell if it was a man or woman, dead or alive. "Probably just another starved stupid ass," she whispered.

Chapter 2

Earl, Jonsey, and Carl followed the man down the road noticing his slow pace. It was the opportunity they had been waiting for. Taking advantage, Carl closed the distance quickly.... picking up a large, thick branch, he lined up the hit, feeling the vibration as it struck his marks head. "See there, boys...I told you he was an easy mark." Carl said excitedly. The blow struck Gabriel in the back of the head, with a loud thwack, propelling him forward on the asphalt. As he lay there unconscious, bleeding from his nose Carl ripped his backpack open, dumping the contents on the road. Angered by the meager contents (one change of clothing, a lighter, an empty water bottle, flashlight, and wallet), he screamed, cursed, and spat on him. Earl and

Jonsey pointed at Carl, "You dumb hillbilly, you said there'd be food. There ain't nothin here but junk! Now what we gonna do?" "Shush," Carl said. Hearing the sound of water, Carl pointed down the hill.

They dragged his body through the tangle of brush down the hill toward the sound. At the edge of the water, they debated whether to dump him head or feet first. The debate abruptly ceased as two green-eyed demons leaped from the brush, backing them away from the human. Stunned, they looked at each other, wide-eyed with fear.

Griffin placed himself beside the human, with one giant paw placed gently on his back. Sadie nudged him with her head. The human moaned. Baring their teeth, fur raised, they staked claim to the human. The Neapolitan mastiffs watched the bandits run up the hill, through the thick brush, and waited for their mistress to arrive.

Chapter 3

Reaching the bottom of the hill, Ell noticed the dogs watching the hillside. She dug her binos from her pack, scanning for movement. All she saw was tall grass, kudzu, and briers. It was eerily quiet around the creek. The only natural sound was the water flowing sluggishly downstream. Her gut told her something was wrong, but the dogs didn't seem overly concerned. She put the binos back in her pack.

Stopping several feet from the body, Ell eyed the man dispassionately. Dead or alive, he had to be disposed of, like any other piece of filth this world had spawned. She had to get him out of the water. A rotting corpse would draw predators to the homestead and contaminate the water. Sadie nudged the man again, he groaned, that's when Ell knew he was alive.

Damn, damn, dammit! She cursed, grabbing the stranger by the shoulder turning him on his back. Peeling back his eyelids, she waved her hand in front of his face. Nothing. She shook him, yelling, "Hey, mister, can you hear me?" Still nothing. Looking at the dogs, she motioned them to each side of the stranger, held his belt out on each side for them to hold in their mouths, while she grabbed him by the arms. "Pull!" she commanded.

She talked to herself as she paced. "You know we could leave your long-ass here for bear bait. Bear stew sure tastes good with a hunk of cornbread during the winter." With a shake of her head, she continued, "Nope, can't do that." Drawing her eyebrows together, she snapped her fingers. "I know, we'll drag you over to old man Welmer's place in that little valley past his barn. No one lives there anymore," she said.

Her decision made, she strained to pull him onto the cart. She wiped the sweat from her brow with her sleeve, stripped off her outer shirt, and continued in her tank top.

Gabriel heard a woman speaking. He tried to open his eyes, but the pounding pain in his head and behind his eyes was so great he couldn't understand all of her words. All he heard was, "Bear bait...leave your long-ass...in that little valley..." His last thought before blackness overtook him was, "Oh God, she's going to leave me!"

Ell dug through her pack for the extra rope she always carried with her. She attached the rope to the D-rings on the dog's harnesses, next she tied the loose ends to the sides of the cart. They should be able to pull him across the creek toward Welmer's place. This was one of those 'Adapt and Overcome' situations, she thought. "Okay, guys, pull!" she said. The cart didn't budge. Confused, she looked at them.

Both dogs sat on their butts looking toward home. Ell followed their gazes. She tried pulling their harnesses; they wouldn't budge. They dug in their front paws, facing home. "NO! NO! NO! HELL NO! We are not taking him home!" she said raising her voice, her arms spread wide in frustration. Sadie looked at Ell, gave a huff, "Yes, we are!"

Ell paced. She knew without their help; she couldn't lug him to Welmer's. She was tired, hot and hungry. The day was three quarters gone, and there would be no hunting today. Hanging her head, she blew out a long slow, defeated breath. "All right, if he dies or does anything hinky, it's all on you! You got it?" She extended her hand, they stood, leaned into the harness and pulled.

Chapter 4

As they neared the cabin Ell removed the harnesses, allowing the mastiffs to perform a perimeter check. Finding no threats, they returned to Ell's side. Now that they were on level ground Ell continued without their help. She unlocked the door, sent the dogs in before her, pulled the cart in, locking the door behind her. She prepared a bed, water for cleaning his wounds and medical supplies. She unstrapped him, then placed a narrow piece of plywood covered with a folded sheet over the edges of the bed and cart. Using his right arm and belt, she pulled him onto the plywood. With the sheet, she pulled him onto the bed. You are tall, she thought.

"God, you're a mess!" she said to the unconscious man. She reached for scissors to cut his clothes off. She stopped when she realized she had no men's clothes to replace them. They needed to soak overnight to remove the blood stains. "We can't have you stumbling around naked, hurting yourself." she muttered. "But they have to come off."

"Do you have any suggestions? ...NO?" she asked. "Well...I have a solution. You won't like it, though." she continued with a tilt of her head.

Ell rummaged through the storage room, came out with four heavy leather belts, a pair of lamb's wool-lined boots which she cut into strips long enough to wrap around his wrists and ankles. After shortening the belts, she punched holes close to the buckle. She put on a pair of disposable gloves to remove his stiff, sweat-soaked, dirty and bloodied clothes.

Once she had him stripped of his filthy clothes, she covered his lower body with a sheet, changed her gloves and washed the dried blood and dirt from his face. She pinched the bridge of his nose between her fingers, gave it a slight wiggle to check for broken cartilage. It didn't seem broken; it was swollen but centered on his face. Running her fingers from his hairline to the base of his skull, she found a ping pong ball sized knot at the base. There was no blood, a good sign, which explained his lack of responsiveness. She washed his hair as best she could with a washcloth, toweled it dry and finger-combed it away from his forehead. Lifting his eyelids, she checked for pupil contraction by passing a penlight before his eyes.

He moaned, turning his head away from the light. "That's a good sign. You're not brain dead," she muttered. She washed the front of his body, noting several small scrapes and cuts. Rolling him over on his left side, she noticed large bright purple bruises to his ribs, low back, and right hip. She pressed her fingers over the bruises, feeling for protrusions pressing the skin outward. "Bruised for sure, maybe cracked," she said out loud.

Refilling her water bucket with clean water, she leaned beside his right ear, saying,

"Your ribs on the right are bruised maybe cracked. I have to roll you on that side to finish cleaning you. If you can hear me, know this will hurt. We'll be as quick as possible."

Calling the dogs to the bedside, Ell had them place their heads against his shoulder and hip. After placing her hands on his sides, she told them to push, rolling him on his right side. The dogs held him while Ell finished her task. She noticed his breathing had become labored, quickly she commanded, "Down easy." while she held his sides. "Thanks, guys," she told them once he was lying on his back.

Amazingly, most of his injuries were minor; a busted nose, small scrapes, cuts, both eyes blackened and swollen. The knot at the base of his skull and the ribs worried her. The ribs would make movement and breathing painful. His vital signs were normal. His lungs sounded clear. Ell stood to stretch her cramped, stiff muscles. Then she wrapped strips of lambs-wool around his wrists and ankles, applied the belts, fastening him to the bed. To reduce the swelling, she laid a clean, cool, damp cloth over his eyes and nose.

Ell picked up his dirty clothes, placed them in a bucket with cool water to soak. After putting away the unused supplies, she went out on the porch to think. What do the dogs sense in him? What am I not seeing? These unanswered questions made her head hurt. As she rubbed her temples to ease the pressure. She mumbled to herself on the way to the kitchen, "I might as well fix him some broth, he's obviously dehydrated."

Chapter 5

Ell pressed a panel on the wall in the kitchen. A slight click was heard as it sprang open. She flipped a switch at the top of the stairs, led lights lit up the dark, cool interior of her extended pantry. She walked down the center aisle until she reached a shelf labeled "Soups/Broths/Stews." From the shelf, she pulled down beef broth, mixed stew veggies, and venison stew meat. Supper would be a simple, hearty meal. She placed a large pot on the stove, poured in the contents of the jars, and heated the stew to boiling. She removed a cup of broth for him, added a cornstarch slurry, to thicken the stew. Twenty minutes later, supper was ready.

Using a serving spoon, she filled a mug for herself and the dogs. After finishing her meal, she carried the broth into the room where the man lay motionless. Standing beside the bed, she watches his chest rise and fall with a slow even rhythm. She let her eyes wander over his face. His jaw was relaxed underneath a scraggly gray-streaked beard. He was wide at the shoulders with long, strong muscular arms. As her eyes traced the thin line of dark hair to his navel, her breath quickened as she remembered the feel of his lean muscles under her fingertips. Memories of the beating she'd received by her husband's hands flashed through her mind. She shuddered hardened her heart and approached his bedside.

Replacing the cloth on his face after rinsing with cool water, Ell parted his lips slightly, dripping broth to wet them. He licked the moisture from his bottom lip, drawing it between his teeth; opening his right eye, blinking to clear his vision. Who was this woman with the long coffee-colored braid draped over her shoulder, he wondered? She watched him with eyes as blue as the sea that pierced his soul.

His voice raspy, throat raw, he asked for more. She obliged, "A little at a time. I don't want you to throw up," she said softly as she placed the spoon to his lips. The warm, savory broth soothed his parched throat.

He looked down at his hands to see why he couldn't lift them. With surprise and shock, he strained against his bonds asking, "WHY?"

Because you need to lie still, you were hit hard on the back of your head, and you have bruised, possibly cracked ribs, which need time to start healing. Head injuries can have complications. I couldn't risk you further injuring yourself." she told him.

Looking down at his feet, he asked, "Who removed my clothes?"

"I did. They were filthy and blood-stained: I have them soaking in cool water," she replied.

"Why am I a prisoner? he asked.

You're not a prisoner, and this is for your own good, she explained again. I will remove these tomorrow if you have no complications during the night. I have expended way too much energy on you today for you to undo all my efforts," she calmly replied.

Ell asked him a series of questions; what his name was, did he remember what happened to him, how much pain he was in.

Before he answered her questions, between sips of broth, he asked her, "Who are you? How did you find me?"

"You may call me, Ell," she replied.

"I didn't find you; they did," she said, motioning toward a dark corner of the room. "Come," she said. The mastiffs walked to the side of the bed, sitting at her feet. "For some reason, they wanted me to help you. It's the first time they've ever refused to help me dispose of trespassers," she said. His eyes widened. "Don't worry, it's not like I'm Kathy Bates or anything," she said.

Hesitantly he answered her questions. "My name is Gabriel. I was trying to get back home, to Birmingham, ran out of food and water, then I was attacked by three men who had been following me. I remember the pain in my head and someone talking about bears...hauling me off to some valley." he answered watching her for a reaction. "Was that you?" he asked. With a single nod of her head, she turned and left the room. "Wait," he called after her.

Chapter 6

As Gabriel lay on the bed, he replayed the

conversation with Ell. She had rescued him and provided him with medical care, food, and water. She had shown no aggression although she had restrained him. He understood lying sill to allow his ribs to heal and he was in considerable pain. How much harm could he cause her in his condition? Who had hurt her? How long had she been living here alone? How had she survived alone? All these questions plagued his mind causing a pounding headache, which distracting his mind.

Suddenly he realized he had to pee. "Shit with my hands tied how am I going to hold it? Please, God, don't let me urinate on myself!" he prayed out loud. Gabriel felt a warm rush of air against his cheek. As he turned his head, he came face to face Sadie's shadowed form, almost touching his face. The dogs she had left them in the room with him. Adrenaline pumped through his veins; elevating is heart and breathing. As he watched, the larger dog left the room while the less large one sat at his side. He could tell by their shadows; these were not your run of the mill dogs.

Sadie sensed something was wrong with the human. She walked to his side and breathed in his scent, looked at Griffin, and gave a low rumble in her throat. He stood and left the room in search of Ell.

Gabriel cleared his throat and called out to Ell, "Miss...Ell...." He waited and listened for a reply. All he heard was Sadie's slow deep breaths, in... out, in... out. He was unnerved by her nearness and steady gaze. The silence frayed his nerves causing him to flinch when Ell asked, "Are you alright?'

Chapter 7

Ell left the dogs with him while she brought in the solar shower bags. She was so tired, all she wanted was a long hot soak in the tub. She emptied two of the bags into the tub, added Epson salt and jasmine oil. Stripping, she submerged her tired aching body into the fragrant, steaming water, leaned her head back, closed her eyes and sighed.

When Ell's skin was puckered, she dried off and dressed. At sixty-one, she was still attractive. She had come to her grandfather's cabin two years ago to heal and hide from the madness of society. She hid from men who hurt women. Her grandfather had left her the cabin in his will. This was home, her sanctuary.

On her way to her bedroom, Griffin met

her in the hallway. He huffed, turned and headed toward Gabriel's room. She followed.

"Are you alright?" she asked from the doorway.

Gabriel flinched at her soundless approach.

"Well, are you alright?" Ell asked.

"Yes.... No!" Gabriel stammered.

Gabriel's face reddened, "I have to use the bathroom!" he pleaded. She nodded. "Watch him," she commanded. "If you make any threatening moves, they will attack," she told him. Nervously, he nodded. Ell removed the restraints, helped him sit up on the side of the bed, pulling the sheet around him as he did so. The sharp pain in his side caused him to grunt with his efforts. Ell stood by to offer help if needed. "If you aren't dizzy, follow me," she instructed. Gabriel nodded, took a breath and stood.

Sadie and Griffin watched from the doorway. As Ell turned to leave, Gabriel asked, "What about them?".

"They stay with you. You do your

business... then go back to bed, Gabriel!" tiredly, she said.

Eyeing them from his peripheral vision, he relieved himself.

Gabriel eased past the dogs, retracing his steps to his bed. He whispered a prayer of thanks, "Thank you for saving me." Sadie raised her head, padded to him and nudged his hand with her muzzle. She nudged him again, and he tentatively placed his hand on her head, stroking her velvety soft fur. She leaned into his hand. Her long drooping ears hung below her jaw, and her skin slid back and forth over her powerful body. Chuckling, Gabriel thought she had twice the skin she needed. Content, she lay at his bedside. Yawning widely, he closed his eyes and slept.

Ell noticed the room was growing colder. Getting out of bed, she pulled two of her Grandmother's thick quilts from a trunk. The quilted tops were pieced with soft blue cotton and backed with tan wool. She placed one on her bed, then covered Gabriel with the second. She placed the soft cotton against his body. She noticed Sadie sleeping on the floor beside his bed. She returned to her bed. Fatigue claimed her as she curled under the warmth of the quilt.

Chapter 8

Ell sat on the porch drinking her morning coffee. Gabriel had been at the cabin for four weeks now. She wondered how much longer he would stay. His wounds had healed along with the return of his strength. Surely, he wouldn't leave during winter. She realized she didn't want him to leave. Was it loneliness or attraction she felt for him? Both maybe. He had a ready smile. Always helped with the chores. Some nights they would sit around the supper table and talk.

He was an open book about himself. She had learned Gabriel had been a construction worker before SHTF. He'd worked in Mobile when the poop sprayed. He had never married, wasn't prepared like some of his buddies. They all lived out of state. They had gone one way, he another. He was an only child; his parents had passed away several years ago, leaving him with no one to go back to. He'd grown up in the city, knew little of gardening, had some firearms training and had done a little hunting in his youth. He was an intelligent, hard-working, handsome man, with a deep baritone voice that quickened her heart when he laughed. On days they worked side by side; he would brush her hair from her face when it escaped its braid. His touch was soft and gentle, at other times like static, thrilling through her body. Lately, the desire for him chased away her nightmares.

Lost in her thoughts, Ell didn't hear Gabriel walk out on the porch until he wrapped a scarf tightly around her shoulders, letting his palms rest on her shoulders. "It's cold out here, you'll get sick," he told her. Together they went inside.

Chapter 9

As Gabriel's strength returned, he was insistent on helping around the cabin. It wasn't right for Ell to work so hard. Through the weeks, she had shared some details about herself.

She had told him she had been a nurse before the event; she had no children, never mentioned a husband. Her parents had passed when she was young leaving her grandfather to raise her. He had lived in the cabin all his life; now it belonged to Ell. He, her grandfather, taught her to garden, hunt, fish, and preserve food. She knew how to live in this new world, a world without electricity, grocery stores, pharmacies or gasoline. He had so much to learn if he wanted to survive. She was a gracious teacher.

When she smiled, really smiled, her eyes sparkled like gemstones. When she laughed at some antic of the dogs, it was light and musical. He wished those smiles and laughter were directed toward him, more. At first, she would shoot daggers at him, when he would brush her arm or hand with his. But now, she didn't withdraw from his touch. Still there was something she kept hidden. She had captured his heart. Gently, he pursued her.

At supper that night, Gabriel decided to test the waters with some neutral questions. "Ell, tell me about Sadie and Griffin?"

"I got them from a rescue shelter before they were put-down. Everyone was afraid of them because they hated MEN. They adopted me, really. They're brother and sister, full-blooded Neapolitan mastiffs from Italy. They are naturally quiet, intelligent, loyal, powerful and protective. I got them about six months before coming here…. Why?" she said.

He carefully replied, "I was curious. I've never heard of them, much less seen one. Do they all have so much skin, large heads, and slobber so much?"

She laughed, "Yes, the standard is lots of

loose wrinkles, large heads. They have always reminded me of lions, in how they sort of saunter when the trot." Pausing, she said, "I still can't believe they accepted you into our little pack."

"So, how long has your little pack been here...alone?" he probed.

Ell hesitated, looking down at the tablecloth she picked at a loose thread before answering. "Two years.... They were all I needed," she said as she stood gathering dishes from the table, so she wouldn't have to look into his magnificent dark chocolate eyes.

Gabriel gathered some of the dishes, followed her to the sink, cutting off her escape. "Please, don't run from me, Ell," he whispered into her ear. His breath warm upon her neck. He inhaled her scent and swallowed hard to keep from crushing her against his body.

"Why won't you trust me?" his words brushed her cheek.

Ell didn't turn; she couldn't. His hot sweet breath upon her neck sent shivers through her body. For so long, she had held her secret close. This man, with his open heart, would be disgusted if he knew what she had allowed to happen. He was a good man, could he handle the truth, or would he leave her? Might as well find out now, she thought. Sitting the plate, she had been scrubbing down, she drew in a steadying breath.

She said, "I've done a terrible thing; actually, I allowed it to happen."

"Go on," he whispered, moving close enough he could feel her body trembling.

Gathering her courage, she said, "I was married. He was an alcoholic, addicted to painkillers. I worked at a nursing home, where they had narcotics. When he ran out of drugs, he tried to force me to steal from my patients. I refused. And in a drunken rage, he beat me until I was unconscious. I was nothing more than a bloody heap on the floor. That's where I got this scar over my left eye. He left me to die, Gabriel. I laid on that floor for two days. Pointing to Sadie and Griffin, she said, "They laid beside me until I was able to crawl to my feet."

Ell, he said softly, "That wasn't your fault. He was the one to blame."

"That's not the horrible part; it's what caused it." she stammered, tears pooling on her lower eyelids. "When my husband, Robert, came home to finish the job, they attacked him. I didn't stop them. I let...them... kill... him. I was glad he was dead." racking sobs shook her body. Shoulders slumped; Ell clung to the edge of the sink waiting for Gabriel to pull away in disgust.

Heartbroken for her, Gabriel pulled Ell into his arms, holding her to his chest while stroking her cheek. As she sobbed, pouring out her anguish. she faced him. "I thought you would leave if you knew I let such a horrible thing happen and be glad," she whispered.

Gabriel brushed her remaining tears away. Placing his hand behind her neck, he tilted her head back so he could look into her eyes. He whispered into her ear, "I'll not leave you, Ell. I want to love you. Will you allow me to do that?" Slowly and delicately, he covered her heart-shaped lips with his. He groaned evidence of his desire pressed into her. He pulled back, waiting for her answer.

"I would like to be loved," she whispered in return. She pressed her lips to his matching her passion to his.

Apocalyptic Winter

About Susan Isenberg

Susan is the mother or two, grandmother of three. She's a semi-retired nurse and has always had a preparedness mindset and a problem solver by nature. Hunting, fishing, gardening and food preservation are a way of life, not a hobby.

She shares from experience what it is like to be hungry and scared for your life.

She is a survivor.

EDGE OF DESPAIR

By Theresa Shaver

Ashley kept her head down and her eyes closed, squinting to see against the icy pellets that bombarded her. With her shoulders hunched she was bent almost in half, trying to push against the driving force of the wind. Each staggering step was pure agony as the gale cut through her many layers like a frozen knife. She was bone-weary with exhaustion but knew that stopping would mean a quick death; and her dying out here would mean a long, lingering death by starvation for her eight-year-old sister, Lucy. And that was something Ashley could not accept.

The toe of her boot caught a rigid object frozen in the ice—sending her sprawling forward onto her chest with a grunt of pain. The canvas bag clutched in her gloved hands flew ahead of her, spilling its precious contents out onto the snow when she tried to break her fall. The sharp pain in her right knee didn't even register against the panic she felt over possibly losing the meager amount of food she had scavenged after six hours of searching that day. Gasping for air through the tightly wound, ice-crusted scarf covering most of her face, she crawled towards the fallen bag to snatch up the desperately needed items.

A frozen wrinkled potato, two withered old carrots, a small package of rice, and one can of black beans long past its expiry date went back into the bag. A glimmer of gold off to her left had her reaching for the final item she had found that day.

It was a painted ceramic Christmas tree. An item that made no difference in their chances of survival but might lift Lucy's spirits. Her sister didn't even know that it was Christmas Eve as marking the months by holidays had been replaced by getting through the days alive and fed.

Ashley pushed her freezing body painfully to her feet and stumbled forward. Her right knee throbbed with every step making walking in the snow even more of a challenge. The icy blowing snow pelted her and when she fell for a second time after only managing twenty feet, she knew she would need to find shelter to take a break and warm up or she wouldn't make it back to Lucy at all.

Getting back on her feet and moving again took a herculean amount of effort. She veered to the right, leaving the street, and stumbled over the snow-covered curb onto the sidewalk. Struggling through the snow as she walked, she passed by the first few businesses with their front windows smashed out, looking for a place that would protect her from the elements. She finally came to a fabric and craft store that had an intact window even though the door had been kicked in. Ashley doubted if there were very many doors still secured in her town as the soldiers had been very thorough in their search for people and supplies. There was a small drift of snow in the front entrance that was keeping the door propped open which she kicked away before closing the door and shoving a small display rack against it to keep it closed and the wind-driven snow out.

Turning from the door, she scanned the store, taking in the tables full of bolts of fabric and the shelving holding sewing, knitting, and crafting supplies. Moving slowly in her frozen state she made her way deeper into the store until she reached one of the fabric tables. Using her arm, she swept half the bolts to the floor and nudged them under the table with her boots. Using the remaining bolts of fabric, she unpinned them and rolled them out until they draped over all sides of the table, reaching to the floor and creating an enclosed space that would be easier to heat. Shrugging off the small backpack she was wearing, Ashley set it and the canvas bag inside, pushing them through the small opening she had left as an entry, and then dropped down to crawl into her makeshift fort.

Half the fabric bolts she'd pushed under the table worked well as a soft seating area and also got her off the icy cold tile while the other half would be unraveled and used for a blanket of sorts. Once she was situated, Ashley pulled the wool hat and the scarf from her head and face and then used her teeth to tug off the thick gloves. Her fingers were stiff, and numb with cold, as she fumbled with the zipper on her pack and began removing the items she would need.

A small, one-burner camp stove was threaded onto a one-pound propane bottle and lit with shaking fingers after dropping the lighter twice. She hovered her hands over the flames for a few minutes to help thaw them before setting the aluminum pot on the burner. The stainless-steel thermos burned against her bare skin from how cold it was, but she was relieved to see it had done its job when water poured out into the pot. A few ice crystals had formed around the sides but there was enough water to heat and do what she needed it to do.

The next three items were what would make all the difference in raising her body temperature after the water began to steam. Ashley set the three floppy, rubber, hot-water bottles in her lap and waited. As she watched the water in the pot, waiting for the wisps of steam to rise, she thought back to how her mother had always filled one and wrapped it in a towel before placing it in her lap to cozy up with after coming in from a day playing in the snow. That simple comfort her mom had given her as a small child had been the solution to not freezing to death over the last month since full winter had hit. The hot-water bottles had been easy to find in many homes as they had been overlooked by all the looters and scavengers. She and Lucy had amassed twenty of them and filled each one with a cup of steaming water before stuffing the bottles into their sleeping bags. They provided enough warmth through the night to survive the plummeting temperatures in the nest they had created for their home.

The silence in her fort, except for the soft hiss of the camp stove's flames, was soothing after the roaring of the wind through the deserted town. When Ashley leaned forward to place her hands over the warming water the silence allowed her to hear the tiny rattle that came from the deadly secret, she carried in her inside jacket pocket. Guilt and shame immediately washed through her at the noise, but she ruthlessly shoved those feelings aside, reminding herself that the secret was a contingency plan, a solution if the worst happened. She wasn't there yet.

Turning her eyes away from her slowly warming hands above the pot, they landed on the canvas bag. Ashley calculated that she would be able to make a watery soup out of the ingredients that would give her and Lucy two meals at best. That would give them dinner tonight and breakfast in the morning before she would have to go back out to search for more food. She cursed the soldiers who had come to her town, who had stolen the majority of the food and people, just two weeks after the event that had taken all the electronics from her world.

Everything had just stopped working at eleven o'clock on a Tuesday morning in late September. When her school finally allowed them to leave, Ashley had gone and picked up Lucy from the elementary school a few blocks from her own high school and they had walked home together. She had been nervous the first night when her parents hadn't returned from work in the city, but she was a mature girl for fourteen and had a few years of babysitting experience under her belt, so she kept her cool. After the second night alone, she got scared. When five days had gone by without her parents returning, she was terrified.

Lucy had so many questions that she couldn't answer, and she wanted to join in as her sister cried for their parents. Being responsible for Lucy had kept her from spiraling into total despair. Day after day, she watched Lucy revert back to the childish comforts she had outgrown. By the time Ashley came to terms with the fact that her parents weren't coming home, and that they were on their own, Lucy was back to sleeping with her tattered teddy, Boo Bear, and sucking her thumb to fall asleep.

She managed to keep things together for two weeks as the food supplies dwindled. A neighbor had shown her how to access water from the house's hot water tank, but everything was starting to run out when the soldiers arrived in town.

The day they had come, she heard banging and yelling out on the street, so she had rushed with Lucy to the front window to see what was happening. When she saw the uniformed men at the doors of the houses across the street a surge of hope filled her but that quickly morphed into confused fear. The soldiers were dragging people from the homes and anyone who fought back was clubbed with their rifle stocks. Ashley watched in shock as a man was dragged out of a house three doors down. He fought back hard and had put down two of the soldiers when a third calmly lifted his rifle and stitched a line of bullets up his body before turning away and leaving the man where he had fallen, dead.

A sharp whine of terror that was growing louder, broke her from a disbelieving trance. he quickly clamped one hand over Lucy's mouth to silence her and used the other to scoop her up around the waist. Ashley bolted for the stairs to the second level with Lucy's back pressed against her chest and feet dangling. She rushed down the hallway, dropped Lucy to the side, and jumped for the hanging string of the attic's fold-down ladder—not willing to waste time with getting a stool. As soon as the ladder legs met the carpet, she was yanking Lucy back onto her feet and shoving her towards the rungs.

"GO! Go fast!" She urged her little sister in a harsh, whispered tone.

Lucy scrambled up the rungs like a monkey, eyes filled with terror. Ashley followed her up just as fast and had the ladder halfway up when she heard the booming pounding against her front door. Biting back a whimper she finished closing the trap door and yanked the string through the hole so no one could pull it back down. The small hook that secured the door would be no protection if the soldiers made a serious attempt to get it open so they would have to hope they wouldn't be discovered. The booming was muffled but loud enough for Ashley to know they hadn't made it into the house yet. She crawled across the attic floor, snagged Lucy by the wrist and moved them both to the front of the attic space where a louvered vent overlooked the street. She took Lucy by the shoulders and gave her a little shake to break the girl from her fear-induced shock.

Ashley's voice was barely above a whisper as she spoke.

"We must be absolutely silent. If we make no noise and don't move a muscle, they won't find us, and we will be safe. Do you understand?"

When Lucy gave her a trembling nod, Ashley pulled her close and held her tight. They both flinched when the crash of the front door being broken down came but stayed still and silent as they listened to the men below search the house.

The minutes seemed to drag on and on until she heard one of the soldiers yell, "Clear! Pack it up, boys."

Her shoulder's sagged in relief thinking that the words meant they were leaving but the faint sounds of cupboards and doors being thrown open and closed told her they were packing up something else and she feared it was all their food.

Moving nothing but her head, she turned it until she could see a small fraction of the street below. Her neighbors filled the sidewalk in a long line that led to a large truck. One by one, they were being forced into it with nothing but the clothes on their backs. Her suspicions about the soldiers in her house were confirmed when a few of them walked into sight carrying boxes filled with random food items. Not only were they taking the people but all their food as well.

Ashley and Lucy stayed huddled in the attic long after the soldiers had cleared the homes on their street and driven away. It wasn't until after the sun had set that they finally dropped the ladder and crept back down into their ransacked house.

A stinging heat against the back of her hands brought her out of her memories and back to reality when she absentmindedly lowered her hovering hands too close to the now steaming pot of water. A harsh, full-body shiver shook her—reminding her that warmed up hands and fingers wouldn't be enough to stave off hypothermia. She needed to get her core body temperature up or she would continue to drift off—until she was fully gone to its effects.

Ashley shut the burner off to keep the water from coming to a boil and dug into her pack until she found a serving spoon. She had learned the hard way, with spills causing scalded skin, that it wasn't a good idea to try and pour the hot water directly from the pot into the small opening in the neck of the hot-water bottles. Instead, she used the large, oval-shaped spoon to scoop the water and transfer it to the bottles with little to no spillage. That was especially important today as she didn't have the fortitude to go back out into the elements to gather more snow to melt.

With all three of the rubber bottles filled with a few inches of the hot water, she went to work on unraveling the fabric bolts to create multi-layered blankets to wrap around herself. Once she was ready, she dragged all the fabric and bottles with her as she scooted over to lean her back against one of the table legs. Positioning one of the hot-water bottles under her coat and against her back, she leaned against the table leg to keep the floppy bottle flush against her spine for direct heat contact. Ashley toed off her pull-on boots, placed the second hot-water bottle under her socked feet and bundled it all together with some of the fabric. The third bottle rested against her stomach under her jacket with her bare hands holding it in place.

At first, the temperature difference between her frigid skin and the hot rubber of the bottles was painful but soon the warmth began to spread through her. Ashley leaned her head back against the table leg and stared out through the opening of her fort. The front window was still a bright white from the storm, so she knew she had at least a few hours before dark to get warmed up enough to make it the last few miles back to Lucy. She pictured her little sister snuggled up in the tent they had set up on top of the tumbling mats in her high school's gym equipment room and prayed she was safe. They had been forced to leave their home a month after the event began and it was the only place Ashley could think of that no one would ever search for food or other scavenged items.

After the soldiers left, when the two girls had finally descended from the attic, they found all the remaining food in the kitchen gone. After a thorough search of the house, Ashley had discovered two large bags of Halloween candy in the linen closet that her mom must have hidden away so it would not be eaten before Halloween. They lived off of that candy and mini chocolate bars for three days before Ashley felt confident that the soldiers had left their town and it would be safe to leave the house in search of food. Her parents kept an emergency stash of cash in their room, so armed with sixty dollars and an old child's wagon, they set out to the business section of town where the only grocery store was located.

The sisters hadn't left their neighborhood since the power went out, so they were shocked by the destruction they found along the way. Cars and trucks were crashed and abandoned on every street. Windows had been broken in almost all the businesses they passed, and a few places had signs of fire damage. It was beyond belief that their quiet little town now looked like the aftermath of a war zone.

When they stepped through the shattered sliding doors of the grocery store, Lucy had grabbed Ashley's hand and tried to pull her back out while gagging at the stench of rotten food that filled the building. Ashley held firm and took in the destroyed business. The floors were covered in trash and trampled food packages while all the shelves she could see were mostly bare. A flood of desperation filled her. They needed food if they were going to survive. They would have to search the store for anything that was overlooked by the looters and soldiers and hope they found enough to get by for a few days until she could come up with an alternate source. Drawing Lucy closer to her, she tried to explain.

"We don't have a choice, Lucy. We have to go in and search everywhere for food or we'll starve. There's nothing left in the house. The candy's gone. We have to find more food!" When Lucy's eyes welled up with tears, Ashley pulled her into a hug. "I know it's gross and it smells really bad, but we have to if we want to eat." She pushed away from her gently and tugged up the neckline of Lucy's shirt until it covered the smaller girl's nose. "There. Just keep your nose covered as we search, and it won't be so bad."

Lucy's eyes crinkled halfway closed and her voice was muffled through her shirt. "It's a different stink under here. I need a bath!"

Ashley laughed but turned away quickly so Lucy wouldn't see the despair filling her eyes. She had to do better, take better care of Lucy. The fact that she hadn't even thought about keeping her sister clean made her wonder what else she was forgetting to do. Panic climbed up her throat at all the ways she had to be better when it came to taking care of her sister. She wished desperately for her mom to be there with them to take over but her deepest fear was that they would never see their parents again. She was all Lucy had now, so she needed to step up and get the job done.

The girls managed to find enough discarded and partially destroyed packages of food to fill the small wagon after an hour-long search. They stayed away from the rotting meat and freezer departments but still had to bat away clouds of black flies that swarmed the store. Ashley relented and left Lucy at the front of the store to wait as she combed through the rotting remains of the produce section.

She gagged constantly, as she sorted through the decomposing fruits and vegetables, and was rewarded with a few bags of apples and root vegetables that hadn't gone off. After three days of candy and chocolate, her body craved anything green. Nothing green had survived in the store - but the carrots, potatoes, and different types of squashes would be a nice change from the junk they had been consuming.

Walking back to Lucy with the produce bags clutched firmly in her hands, she thought about where to find more food. She wondered if any of the homes with gardens would still have plants growing in them or if they had already been harvested for the season. She added it to her mental to-do list as she deposited the bags on top of the other food in the wagon. As the girls stepped out into the fresh air, a chilly late fall breeze lifted Ashley's long brown hair. A shiver had her thinking about how the weather would change soon and that she would need to prepare them for it.

They managed to stay in their home for two more weeks, with Ashley venturing out daily to scavenge for food and supplies they would need to survive the following winter. Her mind never stopped working and worrying about how to keep Lucy alive and the stress and anxiety were taking a toll on her both physically and mentally. She wasn't sleeping well and the last time she caught sight of herself in a mirror, a stranger looked back. Her blue eyes were rimmed with red and surrounded by deep purple bags of exhaustion. She had never seen her skin so sallow before and the mass of matted, oily, hair that framed it all made her look like she was on the edge of madness.

Ashley's appearance didn't matter to her. Stockpiling everything, she could to keep Lucy alive through the coming winter, did. It was her only focus and goal. She was trudging back to their house pulling a loaded wagon filled with winter supplies when a loud laugh from further down the street had her ducking behind a parked car.

Her heart started to pound erratically in fear as she saw a group of four men leave a house and move quickly to the next. Whoever they were, they were clearly looking for supplies, like she was, and that was a danger.

They were only three streets away from her own home where they would find everything. All she had accumulated over the last two weeks would probably be taken. She stayed crouched down behind the car, cursing herself for not having a backup plan; for her and Lucy to move somewhere else. She needed to get back to the house and move as many of the supplies as she could to a safer place before these men discovered them. Waiting until the group entered a new home before she moved, she ran as fast as she could with the wagon back to her home.

In the end, the two girls had managed to move just over half of the supplies Ashley had gathered by using the wagon and a shopping cart that she had brought home with loot a few days earlier. They made three trips between their house and the school before darkness forced them to stop. The last thing they did before leaving their home for good was to secure a folded note to the fridge door letting their parents know where they could find them if they ever made it home.

After that Ashley was too afraid to venture back out into the town for a week, fearing that the men would spot her and follow her back to where she and Lucy were hiding.

With the food supplies running low though, she had no choice but to go back out to search. The scavenging men had done a good job of picking the abandoned houses clean of anything edible. Ashley spent longer and longer each day to find enough food to feed her and Lucy. She had combed all the nearby businesses and homes, being forced out to the edges of the town to find homes she hadn't already searched.

As the weeks passed and the weather got colder, her exhaustion deepened — and her will to fight for survival lessened. She saw her sister get thinner and thinner until her small arms resembled broomsticks, and her ribs could be felt with every hug given, never noticing her own gauntness. Ashley began to wonder why she was fighting so hard. Was she really saving her sister or was it torture? Prolonging their inevitable death by starvation and the cold.

Ashley blinked a few times trying to rid her eyes of the spots that danced in them from staring at the bright white window for so long and took stock of her body. The hot water bottles had done their job. She wasn't exactly warm, but she was no longer shivering with cold. The thaw of her body had brought out a new concern though. Her right knee was throbbing and after some careful prodding, she felt the swelling around it.

The injury wasn't enough to stop her from getting back to Lucy, as long as she could move, she would never leave Lucy alone - but it would make the next few days scavenging missions nearly impossible. Ashley was already weak from a lack of calories. What condition would she be in after days of not eating anything at all? Would she even be able to make it through a day out in the cold after that?

She reached out and dragged the canvas bag containing the meager food supplies towards her and peered into it again. At best, it would be two small bowls of watery soup for both of them. Dropping the bag in her lap, her hand crept up to her chest and her fingers found the outline of the hard, plastic pill bottle hidden in the inside pocket of her jacket.

Maybe it was time. Maybe it would be better if she crushed up the pills and laced the soup with them. They could enjoy a big bowl each and lay down with full bellies for once. Ashley started to nod slowly. She would melt as much snow as it took to fill every hot water bottle they had, and she and Lucy could snuggle in with full bellies to sleeping bags filled with warmth. She would tell Lucy stories of all the happy Christmases they had with their parents and then present her with the small ceramic Christmas tree. They would fall asleep together, full, warm and with loving memories on their minds. It would be a peaceful way to end this nightmare. A gift almost.

Decision made; a great weight seemed to lift from her young shoulders. She began gathering her supplies and packing them all back into her backpack, including the canvas bag of food. She wanted to be back with her sister now.

Ashley slid on her boots and wound the scarf back around her head and face before pulling on the thick wool hat and her gloves. She pushed her pack out from under the table and after lifting the fabric, rolled her body out into the store as she didn't think her knee could handle crawling on it again. Using the sturdy table for support, she got back on her feet and slung her backpack over her shoulder. Even protected from the wind she could already feel the bone-deep chill of the cold air penetrate her many layers. Scanning the store before leaving, she spotted a pair of discarded sunglasses on the cashier's counter. Snatching them up, she put them on to help protect her eyes from the driving snow and limped to the door.

The moment she moved the display rack she had wedged against the door, the vicious wind slammed it open to crash against the wall. Hunching against the assault to come, Ashley stepped out into the storm and felt the wind cut through her like an arctic-forged sword. She fought against it with every step, determined to get back to Lucy and find the peace she so desperately craved. Visibility was no more than a few feet, but she had traveled this route so many times over the last two months that she could make it to the school with her eyes closed.

The first mile drained so much energy from her and left her feet and hands numb. The second mile was accomplished by sheer willpower to see this journey to its end. Something about the loss of all hope gave her the strength she needed to stagger the last few feet to the school's back door, closest to the gym, and she practically collapsed when the heavy door closed behind her, silencing the relentless cry of the gale.

Ashley leaned against the locker covered wall and unwound her scarf to better catch her breath. With eyes closed and the corners of her mouth lifted in a small smile, she reached up and rested her hand against her chest, feeling the outline of the pill bottle that would be the solution to make all of this go away.

For the first time in three months, she felt the stirrings of happiness. No more cold, hunger, pain, or fear for her and her sister. They would go to a better place. It was the right thing to do for both of them.

Pushing off the lockers, a growing smile of peace on her face, she reached up and removed the dark sunglasses and took a few steps towards the gym only to come to a complete stop when her eyes registered a person standing at the other end of the hallway.

She didn't feel any fear that they had been discovered by someone else. She didn't even care about the danger that might be heading her way from this stranger. It was a crushing disappointment mixed with a bubbling rage that filled her. They had almost made it. They had almost escaped from this hell and now the peace she wanted so badly was being threatened by this intruder. The scream of rage that began rising in her throat to be directed at this destroyer of plans cut out instantly at the five words called out to her.

"Ash? Ashley, is that you?"

Her brain registered her father's voice

instantly but her damaged heart and soul felt nothing of the joy they should. It was too late. HE was too late. She had been pushed too far. Broken into too many pieces for her fourteen-year-old psyche to mend.

"Baby, is that you? I came as fast as I could. I tried to come back to you sooner, but I broke my leg. I couldn't travel until it healed. Ashley?"

The pain in his voice reached a part of her that she thought was dead and her hand dropped away from the hidden solution to all her suffering. As she started walking down the long hallway towards her father, Ashley found comfort in knowing the solution would be there for her and Lucy when the time came again in the future.

About Theresa Shaver

Theresa Shaver is the bestselling Amazon author of the six-book series Stranded and the four-book series Endless Winter as well as a stand-alone novel, Scorched. Her latest release is the first book, The Journey, in a new series – Flare.

You can find links to her work at www.theresashaver.com

DEATH BELLS

By N.A. Broadley

Chapter One

The morning was downright cold. She rested her small hand lightly on the butt of a gun strapped to her side. Bella, the lab mutt, padded beside her. Her eyes darting to and fro, looking for her favorite morning activity—chasing squirrels. Nat's worn boots crunched over frozen leaves, and her toes were painfully cold. There would be snow tonight. She wasn't nearly ready. Soon, the Christmas tree would go up, the tinsel and ornaments strung. In spite of everything she would make Christmas happen for her granddaughters.

She needed new boots. New gloves to replace the worn and tattered ones she wore. There would be no buying anything new. Not for her, not for anyone. New was a thing of the past. She felt the eyes upon her but kept her gaze fixed ahead. Her hand tensed and tightened on the grip of her gun. A chill, matching the morning air, crept over her shoulders and the hair stood on the back of her neck. Bella, sensing tension, let out a soft growl.

'Hush.' Nat snapped. Whether the mutt would listen or not, well, that was anyone's guess. What Nat knew for sure was Bella had a mind of her own when it came to discipline. She thought of her granddaughters. Two beautiful girls now in a world that had self-destructed. They wouldn't have the luxury of new school clothes, cute boots or even a new coat for winter. An ache filled Nat's heart. An ache for all the children who had survived only to have to grow in a world that no longer had compassion, heart or soul.

She had been at Shaw's Grocery store three days ago when at 2:22 pm, when the small town of Hillsboro, NH had went dark. She had been standing in the checkout line with a carriage full of groceries, chatting with the woman behind her in line and planning a cookout for the weekend. As she was mentally checking off items from her list, her phone wailed out an emergency alert. She remembered it was strange; no weather alert had ever sounded like this. And pulling her phone from her purse she saw a message scrolling across the screen. 'This is not a test. Stand by for information to follow.' Glancing around, she saw that all activity stopped. All conversation ceased. She was waiting, waiting for the message to follow. Except it never did. No news. No idea of what had happened. Just dead silence, as she and so many others in the grocery store stared blankly at dead cell phone screens.

She swung the barn door open and stepped to the side, fixing her gaze on the inner darkness. She made a sweep of the room, her eyes taking in the hay bales, the animal stalls, seemingly everywhere at once. Her stomach clenched and her teeth on edge. Danger alerts signaled in her brain. The gun in her hand felt like a heavy block of iron. Her late husband's gun. She had other smaller, lighter guns but chose to wear his. She'd probably not hit the broadside of a barn if she needed to, but it was the comfort of the cold steel in her hand that kept her strapping it on every day.

She saw him, crouched low behind a bale of hay. Raising her gun with a shaky hand, she set the sight on him. "Who are you?"

Holding her breath, she watched as he slowly rose. Behind him were two children, a boy, and a girl, both grasping onto his legs fearfully. Nat scanned the room then set her gaze upon the stranger standing before her. His expression was one of fear, desperation, and sadness. "Don't shoot. Please, don't shoot."

"I won't ask again. Who are you?"

The man took a tentative step forward and spread his hands, palms up as if pleading. "My name is Ross. These here are my grandkids. Don't shoot, please. We just needed shelter for the night."

"I ain't gonna shoot you." She lowered the gun slowly and set it back into the holster attached to her belt. Glancing at the kids, she shook her head sadly. Dirt stained faces stared back at her. Hollowed out eyes and weary little bodies. She led them from the barn out into the weak, autumn sunlight. "Where are you coming from?"

Ross sighed tiredly and wrapped an arm around the little blonde-haired girl who clung to his leg. "We ran out of gas about five miles back. Coming out of Claremont."

Nat nodded. Those kids had quite the walk. Claremont was in the valley, and everything from it was uphill.

"I hate to ask, but do you have water? The kids are thirsty. We ran out yesterday afternoon. I can pay you for it."

Her lips curled into a sarcastic smile. Money? That was of no use now. "I have water. When was the last time these little ones had a meal?"

Ross looked at her, and his face reddened. All they'd had in the car was a few small bags of raisins, a bag of chips and one bottle of water. He should have prepared better. He should have done a lot of things better. "Yesterday morning. We ran out of snacks before noontime."

Turning to the boy, Nat knelt in front of him and smiled into his brown eyes. "You see that building over there?" she asked, pointing to the left of the cabin.

The boy nodded.

"Well, I haven't gathered this morning's eggs. Why don't you take your sister and get them? Then we can have some breakfast."

Caleb's eyes light with relief and happiness. He looked over his shoulder at his grandfather for permission.

"Go ahead, Caleb. Take Sarah and do what this nice lady asked."

Like a shot, the boy, Caleb, dragging his younger sister by her hand, ran off toward the chicken coop. Bella, sensing the excitement barked and sprinted off after the kids. She smiled as she watched them go. Standing up, she turned to Ross.

"I'll feed you and the kids, give you a few bottles of water, a can of gas. Then you can be on your way."

Ross nodded gratefully. Last night he had worried endlessly as to how he was going to find food and water. Not so much for himself but for the kids. He was getting desperate enough that he had been thinking of breaking into some stranger's house and taking what he needed for the kids. The walk from where the car had run out of gas had been long. Neither Caleb nor Sarah had complained, but he could see in their eyes the toll it had taken on each of them.

"So, what was Claremont like?" Nat asked, interrupting his thoughts as she walked toward the back porch where a pot of coffee was brewing over an old, Coleman camp stove. The smell made her mouth water. She felt luckier than most. As a homesteader, she lived a tough life filled with hard work and self-reliance. This event, whatever the hell it was, wouldn't change her life much. Albeit, minus electricity, and even that she had covered with a generator and oil lamps, a cold cellar to store perishables and plenty of home-canned foods to keep her and her family from hunger for a long time to come.

Ross shook his head and grimaced. "It was bad. I should have left sooner with the kids. But I thought help would arrive, the power would be restored, and all would go back to normal." Nat nodded. Many people thought help would arrive and that would be their downfall.

"People were panicking. Stores were starting to run out of food, and gas stations closed, and then the looting started...and the gunshots. The kids and I hunkered down at the motel we'd been staying at. Then yesterday the motel was starting to stink badly, no running water, no flushing toilets. People barging in and out, smashing windows, lighting fires in the parking lot, looting and fighting among each other. The kids were terrified, and frankly, so was I."

Nat grimaced as this news settled slowly on her heart. It didn't surprise her in the least to hear this. The cities, in any crisis of this magnitude, would be the first to fall, to fracture and come apart at the seams — too many people and not enough resources. Many would die as food and water ran out. Many would flee the cities and head for the smaller towns and then to the rural areas looking for relief. They would become refugees who would overwhelm many of the smaller town's limited resources thus creating more problems. From there, the issues would only multiply as town after town would turn the refugees away and barricade against the starving masses. The countdown had begun, and Nat could envision the problems that lay ahead for them all.

She moved slowly, tiredly as she poured herself and Ross a cup of coffee. Was she prepared enough for what was happening? What had happened? Did she have enough food to get through the next few months if this event lasted that long? Even though her larder was full, she couldn't help but worry. She had laid out bait for the bear that she knew had a den nearby. Hopefully, she'd be able to hunt later today and add bear meat to her larder. She expected her son and his family, her daughter and her daughter's husband to show up at the homestead at any time. Did she put enough away for all of them? And what about the stragglers? Defenses would be put into place. And the freezer, it was full of meat that she would have to can to preserve. The list was endless.

Squeals of joy brought Nat from her long thoughts as Caleb and Sarah ran happily toward her, Bella bouncing along behind them joyfully as she followed her newfound friends. Their little hands clutched around the eggs they gathered.

Running up to Ross, Sarah smiled happily as she showed him her bounty before handing them to Nat. "Grampa! Look, eggs!"

Ross smiled softly and nodded. Nat could see the shadow of sadness behind his smile. "Okay kids, there's a swing out back. Why don't you play while Grampa and I fix breakfast?"

After they ran off, Nat busied herself on the makeshift plank table that held the camp stove. In one pan bacon sizzled while in another pan she cracked the eggs and scrambled them. With a large silver serving spoon she slowly stirred a pot of bubbling oatmeal. Ross set the picnic table with plates, forks, and bowls. She drew the purple scarf she wore tighter around her neck to ward off the chill. "So where is home?"

Ross gazed off toward the fields and woods. "Concord."

"And the kid's parents? Are they in Concord waiting?"

"No." Ross replied with a grimace. "They are in New York, a weekend getaway. It was Sandy's idea, my daughter. She wanted to surprise Ned, her husband with an early birthday celebration."

A sad sigh escaped Nat's lips. New York. She couldn't even imagine what had fallen upon that city. Although she didn't say it, chances of Ross's daughter and son in law making it out of that city and back to Concord were slim to none. If a city as small as Claremont was tearing itself apart at the seams, what chance did New York have of surviving?

Scolding herself for prying, she scooped the eggs and bacon onto the plates. It wasn't her concern nor her business. She had her own to take care of. She didn't need Ross's problems.

"I'll pack you some food for the trip. Give you enough gas to make it home. Do you have a weapon?"

"No. I've never had need of a weapon!" Ross snapped in frustration.

Angrily, Nat rolled her eyes and sighed heavily. She then snapped back. "Do you know how to use a gun even?"

A weapon. A gun. He was a history teacher for God's sake. Never once had he even thought about owning a gun. Never once had he ever thought he would need a weapon.

Sane, liberal history teachers did not carry guns. He lived in a quiet community. Flowers grew on every lawn. Weekend bar-b-ques with the neighbors. Pool parties and golf. White-collared polo shirts and sneakers. What he'd seen in the last three days spun crazily in his mind. And he had no idea of how to handle this. "No."

A groan of frustration choked in Nat's throat. How could anyone be so clueless? So unprepared? "Well? You better start thinking about defense! You've got two little ones depending on you!" she hissed angrily. Turning on her heels, she walked toward the back of the house to where Caleb and Sarah were playing.

"Hey? Time for breakfast." She called out.

The sun warmed the air around them, and while the children cleaned their plates of every morsel of food, Nat sipped her coffee and gazed out over the gardens and fields, the woods and mountains. Her gardens were about done. A few root vegetables still had yet to be dug, and a few tomatoes still clung stubbornly to the vines. Pumpkins and hard squashes had a bit longer to go. Thankfully she had put by most of the garden before the power went down.

"Kids? Why don't you both go play while Grampa and I get some things done," she suggested as she sent them out of earshot. Turning to Ross, she took her holster from her belt, withdrew her gun. There was no safety to check. It was an old six-shooter.

"This is gonna be quick and dirty, but I just can't send you out on the road with no way to defend yourself." She said as she handed him her gun. She watched as he tentatively grabbed it. For the next twenty minutes she instructed him how to load, unload, pull back the hammer and shoot. Their target was a pumpkin Nat had set up on a fence post fifty feet away. After she felt reasonably comfortable with his handling of the gun she handed him her husband's gun and had him attach the leather holster to his belt. She hadn't wanted to give up her weapon but she had others, plenty of others, which she could use.

Leaving him to watch the kids she made her way into the house. "I'll pack you and the kids some food and water."

An old backpack hung in the attic, and she grabbed it down off of its hook. Looking at it brought back warm memories of the first time it had been used by her grand-daughter on her very first day of school. Minnie Mouse stared back at her, and she smiled. She didn't suppose Ross would care about carrying a Minnie Mouse backpack, at least Sarah would probably like it. Taking it into the kitchen she packed it with several bottles of water, a few snack packs of crackers and cheese, some dried fruit and a couple of freeze-dried meals that were part of her food prep storage. Even though it wasn't much, it should get them through the day.

She thought about some of the hazards they might run into trying to make it into Concord. It wouldn't be an easy journey. People were getting to the point of desperation now.

She didn't have to see this to know it. It was just the fact of the matter at hand. She hated herself for turning Ross and the children away. But what choice did she have? If she let them stay, then she would inevitably run out of food and supplies for her own family sooner. Shaking her head, she slung the pack over her shoulder.

"Remember. If anyone approaches your car or tries to stop you, you don't let them! You can't second guess this Ross. Those children depend on you to keep them safe." She warned as she walked with them to the end of the driveway. Ross nodded.

"We'll be fine. And thank you for all you've done," he murmured. Nat smiled sadly. Would they be fine? Would they make it home? A sinking feeling in the pit of her stomach made her think not. She watched the three of them walk down the tar road until they were out of sight.

∞

A glance at the sun's position in the morning sky gave Nat a sense of urgency. She had spent hours with Ross and the children, hours that she had planned on using to create defensive perimeters for her home. Walking quickly to the barn, she grabbed the chainsaw and rifle. One thousand feet of her property edged the road. And although it was a back, mountainous road, it was still vulnerable to accessing her property. Her plan was too lay a barrier of downed trees along that road frontage and nest in barbed wire. Following that, she would move in about twenty-five feet, and place bear boards, her secret weapon, a series of two by four boards with nails/screws pounded up through. She would cover those with thick leaves, and even those with the thickest soles on their boots would feel the pain of these bear boards if they stepped down on them. Would these things stop an intruder? Probably not, but it sure would put a hurt on them and give her enough time to prepare for an intruder.

The third line of defense would be a series of punji stakes, trenches dug into the ground, with sharpened sticks concealed inside of the trenches. This line of defense would create crippling harm to anyone who stepped into these traps. Then lastly, fishing line strung from tree to tree with tin cans filled with pebbles. Crossing these lines would set off enough noise to alert her of an intruder. Today she had her work cut out for her.

Just as she crossed over to the southern

edge of her property, Nat stopped, cocking her head to the side. A vehicle, loud and fast, was heading for her driveway. Behind it, under the noise of a screaming engine, she heard a dull roar. Turning, she lifted her rifle and peered through the scope. Her breath stopped, and a wave of fear engulfed her. She watched as the car came to a screeching halt and the passenger door flew open. Nausea spread up into her throat as she saw Caleb and Sarah come tumbling out of the car door. Behind the car were two motorcycles and as the kids rolled across the dirt driveway, she saw the car back up and collide with the motorcycles. Screams, glass shattering, and gunshots assaulted her ears as the situation unfolded. Stunned, it took her a few too many precious seconds to react.

Taking a deep breath to calm herself, she set the sight of her gun on one of the motorcyclists. Holding her breath she squeezed the trigger and watched as the bullet hit dead center of the faceplate on the helmet collapsing the person onto the hard-packed dirt. Moving her gun to the left brought the second attacker into her line of fire. She squeezed the trigger again and saw her bullet send up a puff of dirt, missing him. She watched him dive for cover behind a tree. Wiping the sweat from her brow with a shaking hand, she aimed again. The attacker was tucked out of sight, but she could make out the tip of his black leather boot. Drawing in a deep breath she set her sight on it and tapped the trigger. As the bullet hit its mark she saw the black boot jump with impact and then heard the scream of pain that followed.

"C'mon you fuck...move out...." she hissed.

Waiting for what seemed an eternity but in actuality was only a few seconds, she saw the attacker bend and grab at his foot. This move allowed her to aim in on his chest and she took the opportunity, tapping twice, sending him to meet his maker. Turning her head, she bent as her stomach erupted, and she spewed her morning breakfast onto the dark, leafy soil. Shaking, she wiped a hand across her mouth and made her way toward the children as tears of anxiety mixed with horror, spilled from her eyes. She had just shot two men. Never in her life had she thought she would be capable of committing an act such as this.

With quick long strides, she made her way to where the children were wrapped up in each other's arms beside the car.

Sobs met her ears as she bent down.

'Caleb? Sarah? It's okay. You're safe. It's okay.' She murmured softly as she gathered them into her arms. Gazing over the tops of their heads she spied Ross slumped back in the seat. "Shit."

"Caleb? I need you to be strong for me? Can you do that?" She whispered. Caleb nodded.

"I need you to take Sarah and go to the house. Please. Just go to the house, and I'll be there shortly." She didn't want either of them to see their grandfather all bloodied up like he was.

"But what about grandpa?" Caleb asked. A fresh wave of tears filled his eyes.

"Don't worry. I'll be with grandpa. You need to help me with Sarah right now okay?"

She watched as Caleb grabbed his sister's hand and began walking toward the cabin. When they were on the front steps, she then turned to the car. She crawled insider and felt her stomach sink.

"Oh Ross...damn it, man!" she moaned as she gazed into his eyes. Blood was trickling from the corner of his mouth, foaming with each tortured breath he struggled to take. His body had been peppered with broken glass, the fragments twinkling in the sunshine like some garish red rubies as blood seeped onto them from two wounds in his chest. There was nothing she would be able to do to help him. Squeezing his hand she spoke softly. "I'll stay with you until you cross over."

Ross opened his eyes and struggled to speak. "You take care of my babies...promise me...promise me!" he gurgled. Nat's eyes filled with tears.

"I will; I promise Ross. I will."

His hand, clasped in hers, slid limply away. She bit down on the scream of pain as it built up behind her throat as the truth of it all hit her. People killing each other. This in just two lousy days? Fight or die. In all her fifty-plus years, she had never even thought about taking another's life, and now, just in the last fifteen minutes she had not only taken one life but two. With a weary and heavy heart, she climbed out of the car and made her way slowly back to the cabin. There were two children waiting for her — two children, waiting for their grandpa who would never come back. Her heart crushed with silent tears.

"And so the death bell tolls."

Nat entered the cabin and looked at Caleb and Sarah sitting on the couch. Reddened eyes from crying, curled into one another as if hanging onto a lifeline. She knelt before them, her knees cracking and popping as if singing their tears into the room.

"Where's grandpa?" Caleb asked as he disengaged himself from Sarah's arms.

Nat sighed and shook her head.

"He's behind you, right? He's coming right?"

What could she say? Her words had run out. Nothing that would ease their pain passed through her lips. Only tears that filled her eyes, only a shake of her head.

"I hate you! I hate you! It is all your fault!' Caleb yelled as the truth dawned on him. He exploded up off of the couch and launched himself at her. She folded him into her arms as his small fists beat at her sides and back.

"I know Caleb. I know. I hate me too." She whispered as he struggled against her. Sobs shook his thin shoulders and wracked his body. Tears soaked her shirt front. Waiting, she held him until he quieted and then pushed him gently back toward the couch. It was her fault and guilt chewed gravely at her gut. Turning she walked back out of the house to the front porch and leaned against the wall, then sank slowly to the floor. Curling her knees up, she embraced them with her arms and sobbed quietly. Lack of sleep, stress, worry, and fear were beginning to take their toll on her.

Three dead bodies in her driveway, two children who were thrust into her life. And haunted by the words Caleb had spoken. It was her fault. None of this would have happened had she just let them stay. Her selfishness had cost Ross his life. She had known how dangerous it was out on the road. She had known he was not skilled enough to protect himself or the children from that danger. And yet she had made him leave. Sure, logically it made sense. To protect and keep what was hers to ensure that her own would be taken care of. But her heart had warned her it was a wrong thing to do. It had been selfish. And she blamed only herself. Never had she hated anyone more than she did herself at this moment. Wiping her face on the sleeve of her shirt, she pulled herself up off of the floor. Self-pity never put supper on the table as her mama used to say.

Caleb glared at her as she explained to him what she needed him to do. His face stony as he grabbed Sarah's hand and led her to Nat's truck. Nat couldn't take care of the three dead by herself. She was neither physically nor mentally strong enough to do that. She would have to go to town and enlist the help of the police. A sarcastic chuckle caught in the back of her throat. Two days ago she would have been able to pick up the phone and dial 911. Two days ago she would have been able to jump on the internet and send out a message for help. Two days ago there would have been an ambulance, police, hospitals and social services available. Where was FEMA, The American Red Cross or perhaps the National Guard? Would anyone arrive and save them? She didn't even know, and she highly doubted it. They, along with millions of others, were on their own.

On day one of the event, she had made her way to the Washington Town Office. She had seen the chaos there as the towns two police officers and the selectmen were trying to make sense of what was happening. Crowds of people loitered in the town common, confused people, angry people, her neighbors, and acquaintances. No one knew what had happened and even worse, what to expect. She hoped that things in town had calmed a bit because honestly, she didn't know where else to turn.

The first flakes of snow drifted lazily toward the windshield as she drove, her heart hammering in her chest. Glancing beside her, she took in the scared faces of the children and smiled to reassure them. Just then the driver's side window shattered, and instinctively she ducked, covering the children with her body as the truck careened out of control. She screamed in pain as her head rocked off the dashboard and the truck slammed into a tree. Pain exploded behind her eyes, and she heard Sarah whimper in fear. She struggled to stay conscious and fumbled for the gun on her side.

Voices, laughter, footsteps as they advanced on the truck. Tears clogged her throat, and she swallowed hard. Save the children! She closed her fingers around the butt of her gun and struggled to untangle herself from Caleb who was slumped over in the seat. Through the haze of blood pouring down her forehead and into her eyes she saw the men approaching. She screamed in fury as one of them; a dark-haired, skinny man smiled in through the shattered glass at her.

"Well, well, what have we got here?" he laughed. Nat swung the gun around and watched his eyes widen in surprise as she pulled the trigger. His face crumpled as he fell. Sucking in a deep breath, pain rocketing through her body, she aimed her gun again and fired until the empty chamber clicked dryly. Panic kept her finger squeezing the trigger and tears of fear and outrage cascaded down her cheeks, mixing with the blood from her head wound. Screams from the kids erupted in the air around her which stank of sulfur and heavy smoke making her cough.

"Get out! Get out of the truck now!" she yelled as she pushed both Sarah and Caleb toward the passenger door. Smoke billowed up from under the hood of the truck, and orange licks of flames rose into the air. She tumbled out onto the ground behind the kids, grasping at the wet, frozen leaves as her head spun in agony. Fighting nausea, fighting her own panicked breaths, she crawled away from the truck. Curling in on herself she sobbed, the sound heartbreaking.

"I don't know how to do this! I can't do this!" she repeated over and over and over, and she rocked back and forth. She sighed softly when a pair of little, warm arms closed around her.

"Miss Nat? Please stop crying; we're okay. Miss Nat, don't leave us," Sarah's voice crooned into her ear. Nat wiped the away her tears and drew a deep, shaky breath.

"It's okay baby. It's okay," she whispered back and looked out into the darkening woods. Whether she could do it or not, she knew for them, for Sarah and Caleb, she would have to. There would be no room for self-pity, no room for giving up. Only determination would get them through. Gritting her teeth, she rose to her feet.

"Okay, kids. C'mon. We've got some walking to do." With that, she turned and grabbed her rifle and her handgun from the smoking truck. God help anyone who dared get in their way.

About N.A. Broadley

N.A. Broadley is the author of the Apocalypse Trail Series and writer of the immensely popular Around the Homestead short stories.

She's also the host of Around the Homestead with Nancy on Prepperpodcast.com.

Nancy homesteads on her 2+ acre farm in western New Hampshire and shares the information she learns.

Follow N.A. Broadley

https://www.facebook.com/NA-Broadley-Author-2315285068538146/

Https://nabroadley.com

MR. MCKEW'S BODY

By Stephanie Mylchreest

Her body ached where the man had touched her last night. In the dim light she looked down at her thighs and saw the red mottling that would soon turn blue and then brown. She pulled the thin blanket up to her chin, covering herself completely, and rolled over onto her stomach. Slowly, she inched towards the window and peered through the gap between the boards that had been nailed to the frame on the other side of the glass. It was dark outside, but beyond the dead street, beyond the lifeless city, the sun was silvering the snow-capped mountains.

How many days had passed since he'd locked her up inside this house? She'd lost count, but it was long enough that Mr. McKew's body had been eaten by predators on his front lawn. Hungry neighborhood dogs had been the first to come sniffing around, nosing under Mr. McKew's dark blue dressing gown. And the crows came and were the ones to finally strip his bones bare. One night — under cover of darkness — the bones themselves had just disappeared.

That's how she'd measured the passing weeks; by the slow and complete destruction of Mr. McKew's body.

As she observed the predators decimation of Mr. McKew, several thoughts simmered inside her, threatening to overboil and leak all over her. She clamped a lid shut on them, but they bubbled away unabated: What had happened to the bodies of her beloved family? Were they safe where she left them? Or were other, more insidious predators returning them slowly to the earth?

The man had taken her into this house soon after the sickness spread to humans. It started as an animal pandemic, killing large swathes of factory-farmed pigs through Asia and Africa. Then the factory workers stared dying, and it spread more rapidly than anyone could have expected. When it reached her town, people panicked. There was a run on the local supermarket. People locked themselves inside their homes trying to escape the sickness.

But it didn't help.

She thought their home would be safe. They had a wide yard filled with pretty trees that lost their leaves in the winter. There was plenty of space between them and their neighbors. And her father watched from behind the drapes in the front window, looking for the sick or infected, his rifle in his hand. "You won't actually shoot anyone, will you?" she asked him.

His eyes were sad when he looked back at her. "Times have changed. Keep away from the windows."

Even though they isolated themselves, it wasn't enough. Or maybe they were already infected, locking themselves in with the very thing they feared. First her mother and sweet younger sisters had died. She couldn't think of them without feeling razor wire in her throat. Her father had been the last to submit, his eyes rimmed in red, coughing up blood. Tears had poured down her face as she watched the virus take him. "What do I do?" she'd begged him. "When you're gone. What do I do? Where do I go?"

"I won't leave you," he'd gasped out. But the truth had flickered across his eyes like a badly kept secret. They both knew.

"Please, tell me what to do. I'm so scared."

"Head out of the city," he told her, each word painstakingly difficult. He had to pause in order to catch his breath. The virus was quickly worming its way through his lungs, filling his respiratory system with mucus and blood. "Don't wait. There are bad people. Head south. I heard there was a settlement there."

But she hadn't listened. She'd waited too long.

After her father died, she wrapped his body in the filthy, bloodstained sheet upon which he had lain in the final death throes of the virus. She pulled him off the bed and dragged his body down the hall. She felt an urgent need to reunite him with her mother and sisters.

Compartmentalization. It was the only was her brain could survive the end of the world.

She didn't have the strength to dig a hole big enough for the four of them. She also didn't dare put her family outside. The thought of some hungry, desperate animal feasting on the flesh of her loved ones was too much to bear. So, she did what she could. One by one, as the virus had ravaged them, beaten them down and finally drowned them in their own bodily fluids, she wrapped them up and dragged them to the basement.

That's where she took her father. She stood at the closed door, his body motionless at her feet, and felt her entire being break apart. She was at once there, her head resting on the heavy green door, her hand poised on the door handle, and at the same time she was somewhere else, somewhere fractured and separate from the terrible reality of her dead family.

Piece by piece, she built herself back together.

Then, she cracked open the door, holding her breath against the terrible odor of death and decay, and pushed her father's body to the edge of the stairs. "I love you, Dad." She then pushed him down, hearing the thump, thump, thump as he moved his way down towards the others.

The door closed heavily, as if announcing the finality of it all.

She needed to move. She needed to get out of the house. She needed to get out of the city. Winter would be there soon. It made sense to travel before there was snow on the ground. Who knows how far she would have to go south before finding others with whom she could take refuge.

She had a sturdy bag, warm clothes, and a gun to protect her.

But she'd stayed too long.

The man came at night. She was in the kitchen, soaking two-minute noodles in cold water, willing them to soften as she prodded them with a serving spoon. She hadn't been careful. She thought everyone in her town was dead; she'd left the door unlocked and a candle burning.

A moth to a flame.

A dog to a bone.

Rough hands grabbed her from behind, a hand wrapped around her mouth to stop her screaming. It struck her as absurd. Who was going to hear her? There was no one left to help.

He hadn't taken her far. He'd set up at Number Eighteen, only four houses down. He must have been preparing for her, because he'd stripped the room. There was a bare mattress on the ground, a thin sheet, no furniture, no books, nothing at all but yellowing walls and peeling paint.

Every morning, as the dull light crept finger by slender finger into her room, he'd slide the key into the lock. "On the bed," he would bark, his pale blue eyes strangely incandescent in the dark.

He would place a plastic children's glass filled with tepid water on the floor. Next to it, he would place a plastic plate. The food was scant, whatever he'd managed to scavenge the day before. "Eat now," he would say, and she would crawl towards the plate and eat and drink. She always rushed the eating, to get the next parts over and done with.

He would be rough, brutal, unrelenting.

He'd broken her.

Or so he thought.

Once he finished with her, he would take the plastic plate, the plastic cup, and the bucket of her waste, which he would empty and toss back inside later. The door would lock with a loud click.

It was the same every day until Mr. McKew's body was gone and the grass began to frost in the mornings.

It was last week when she first heard the screams. He brought the woman to the house in the middle of the night. She peered through the crack between the boarded-up window and saw the blanket of twinkling stars and the bright crescent moon. But they were already inside, and she didn't get to see the woman's face.

But those sounds. Those awful, soul-crushing sounds. They bought her back to life. She was going to get out of there. She would save that woman.

She was going to save herself.

She heard his feet on the landing, the same as always. He walked slowly towards her door, as though taunting her. I'm coming, the creak of the boards seemed to say. I'm coming for you.

"On the bed," came his voice. But she wasn't on the bed this time. She was waiting for him.

She heard the key slide into place, heard the click of the pins dropping. She stood a step back from the door, in the deepest shadows of the room. Her back was pressed against the yellow, peeling wall. The door opened as it always did and suddenly, there he was.

His eyes opened wide in surprise when he looked to the small mattress and she wasn't there. He dropped the glass and plate which he'd carefully balanced on one arm. They landed on the wooden floorboards with a soft clunk. At the same time, she pulled her arm back and swung the bucket at his face. Excrement flew over him, in his eyes, his face. He growled a deep, dangerous growl, and she knew she had to act now. There would be no second chance.

In an instant, she had the sheet wrapped tightly around his face. The image of her father, wrapped in another sheet another lifetime ago, filled her with a strength she didn't know she possessed. She twisted the sheet tightly, blinding him, and pulled him into the room. He stumbled, and she locked her knees before charging into him and sending him flying to the ground.

She turned to the door, her heart pounding wildly, every sense sharpened. The key protruded from the lock in the door. He was on the ground, reaching for the sheet, yelling filthy words at her. She had to get out of there! She lunged for the doorway and her fingers brushed the lock when she felt his hand tighten around her ankle.

"Let me go," she screamed. She kicked her leg back hard and felt her heel connect with something. She heard the strangled cry of pain. He tightened his grip, and she kicked again, and again. Finally, his fingers loosened.

She twisted away and crawled to the door, slamming it shut. She was on her knees in an instant and twisted the key in the lock, shutting him inside.

At the same moment, something with the power of a freight train smashed into the door. Her heart was jack hammering in her chest, and she stepped back as the man charged again and again at the heavy wooden door. It shook and shuddered with every blow, but the lock held... For now.

Her hands were shaking. She stood

momentarily frozen, blood pounding in her ears. Somehow, she willed herself to walk away from the door.

"Where are you?" she called out. She could hear the man screaming obscenities at her, but she continued down the landing, pausing at each door. "Where are you? Please answer me. I want to help you." She paused briefly at each of the doors, listening for a beat before moving on.

She reached the stairs and padded down in her bare feet. The heavy thudding of man against wood continued. Each time he smashed into the door, she feared it would be the last time. "Please, where are you?"

She reached the ground floor and spun around wildly. Where could the woman be? Thump.

To her left there was a comfortable living room. Family pictures lined the walls and an overstuffed sofa faced a dark, flat-screen television. She took in the crochet doily someone had carefully placed under an ornamental lamp, the soft woven rug on the floor. Thump.

To her right was a large kitchen, the cupboard doors hanging open, the shelves stripped bare.

Thump.

"Are you here? I want to help you?"

Thump.

Then she saw it, the basement door. It was the same color as the basement door at home, for a split second detached from the chaos unfolding around her. They had stained the wood dark green, like the fine needles of a Christmas tree.

She scuttled over to the door and shook the handle. It was locked.

Thump.

"Are you in there?" she yelled. She strained for any sound and was about to turn away when she heard it. Someone walking up the stairs behind the locked door, weeping. "I'll get you out," she screamed desperately. "I'll get you out."

She ran back to the kitchen and yanked open drawers at random. She grabbed a handful of implements and moved quickly back to the basement door.

Thump.

She took a knife and wedged it in the lock. She rattled the handle, but it was stuck tight. She leaned her weight against the knife handle, but the lock wouldn't yield. "I'm coming," she called again, frantic. She could hear the woman sobbing on the other side of the green door.

Thump.

She dropped the knife to the ground and scanned the other implements she'd found in the drawer. She selected a corkscrew and stuck the sharp end in the lock, twisting it over and over until — finally — she heard the lock pop.

She put her hand on the green door. For a split second she was back at home, her father on the ground at her feet, his body wrapped in its death shroud. The magnitude of her losses weighed down on her so heavily, she almost disappeared.

Thump... Crash.

"He's coming!"

She yanked open the door, took in the scared eyes, the tangled hair, the desperate expression. "You're safe," she said. "I'll get you out of here." She grabbed the woman's arm and yanked her through the green door. They ran, stumbling over their own feet as they raced towards the front door.

They burst out into the cold morning air just as they heard him yelling from the top of the stairs. They didn't look back. Their legs pounding the ground, their arms pumping, they passed the spot where Mr. McKew had died. Her eyes darted to the flat area of grass where his body lay until the cruel, twisted, beautiful universe had reclaimed it. Then they rounded the end of the street and kept going.

They didn't stop running until they could literally go no farther. Together, they fell to their knees on the grassy sidewalk outside a sweet house with a white fence ringing the front yard.

Finally, she turned to the woman. She was wearing thin pants and a threadbare, oversized gray tank top. Her blonde hair was greasy and hung in tangled strands around her face. But her eyes... her eyes sparkled with life. Her cheeks were flushed pink.

"You saved me," the woman said. "Thank you. I thought I would be locked in that basement forever." She shuddered. "We survived the apocalypse only to be taken by a madman."

She wasn't sure what to say in return, and for a long moment she looked at the frost-flecked ground. Finally, she looked up. "We'll need to get some supplies if we are going to make it out of the city."

"Yes. Hopefully some warm clothes too. A jacket, scarf, sturdy shoes. And some food, of course."

"There have to be some survivors. And I mean good people. People like us. My father told me to head south. Apparently, there is a settlement there."

"I heard about the settlement too," the woman said. "We'll stick together. We'll look out for each other, and we will make it there." The woman paused. "What's your name?"

"I'm Suzy," she said, speaking her name for the first time in months.

Something happened when she spoke the words out loud. Something wonderful. She could feel the warmth, the hope, blossoming from deep in her belly.

"I'm Grace," said the woman.

Suzy and Grace smiled at one another briefly and then stood up.

Their fingers entwined for a moment. They were going to be okay.

About Stephanie Mylchreest

Stephanie writes speculative fiction and dark fantasy in the wee hours of the night, after her children have gone to sleep. She enjoys writing stories about characters placed in highly unusual situations and exploring how they deal with the fallout. Her favourite books include Harry Potter, The Road, 1984, Wool, and Station Eleven. Her favourite movies include the Lord of the Rings trilogy and Back to the Future.

Stephanie has a Master of Laws and a Bachelor of Science, and spent a decade working as a lawyer before pursuing her writing career.

You can check out her Insularity series on Amazon, a late post-apocalyptic cli-fi adventure, and book one in her new series – Dark Resistance – is available now.

You can connect with her on her website: www.stephaniemylchreest.com

There were so many amazing stories that we simply couldn't get them all into one volume.

Coming ★ December 2019

Made in the USA
Monee, IL
14 April 2024

56660519R00156